a cabbage named Fred

a cabbage named Fred

D. I. Richardson

Published through CreateSpace Independent Publishing

Typeset in Baskerville and Chalkduster.

ISBN: 9781700781383

This novel is dedicated to

Blankts, Tülpa, Teddy, Izzard, and Fred

for their gift of music,
and inspiring this novel.

"That's just me against myself again,
   I fight a losing battle.
And I find peace inside the sandbox,
   I'm the princess of this castle.
You'd find pieces of the Barbies,
   sent to death across the gravel.
I'd introduce you to a vegetable,
   who's sweeter than an apple."

A Cabbage Named Fred by Tülpa ft. Blankts

THE SUMMER

ONE

I could start this off by saying I never had many friends in high school, or in elementary school for that matter. I was never a very outgoing kid, but that doesn't mean I'm a lost cause. I'm a great listener, an observer. I spent all my free time in class working and listening to the other kids talk about their adventures. I lived vicariously through those conversations never meant to be heard by me. And I didn't mind it. That was my life, it was who I was, and I liked it. Society might have you believe that you need to talk all the time, but that's not true. Only speak when you have something to say. Listen otherwise. And listen to hear what the other person is saying, not just until you can say something again.

So I listened. And learned. And I observed how people were. And that doesn't mean I was a total loner either. I had friends. Two close friends and a girlfriend (well, I had a girlfriend up until April and it's late June at this point in my story). But this isn't a story about my ex-girlfriend. I just needed it to be out there that I wasn't some horny 16-year-old virgin dying for one night of indelible passion. I had lost my virginity at 15 to a friend and quickly moved on to dating my first serious girlfriend. I was both of their first times. Not that it matters much to me, but it does to some people, and that's alright.

I wouldn't be where I ended up if not for each of those two girls shaping how I view love and relationships, I think. I'm only young still, so I've got a lot of shaping left to do. And again, I was an observer. I grew through eavesdropping on people. And I turned that into a hobby.

I had always found myself interested in writing. Whether it was song lyrics to songs with no music (poems, I guess) or short stories or even half-hearted attempts at novels. I loved writing. I wrote my first short story at 10 years old. It was a Halloween short story for my class. I wrote about a creepy mansion that had a murderer living inside of it, and the group of friends had to escape before they all died. It was titled *McMurder Mansion*. I know, it was truly riveting, but cut me some slack. I was ten.

Over time, my writing flourished though. The more I focused on other people, the more fascinated I got by the way people interacted. The subtleties in their voices and faces when they spoke and told stories. I even tried to focus on the emotions of people when they were crying on my shoulder. (I suppose part of the reason I ever got a girlfriend was because I *actually* paid attention to their emotions, and in my experience, girls are quite emotional.)

It took a long time for me to open up to people about my writing, actually. Writing and drawing seem to be the two art forms that get relegated to notebooks and computer folders and never shared with people. But I did eventually open up. I showed my friends and told people I wrote short stories and poems. I took a creative writing class the year prior to this year and it opened my eyes a lot. And though I had always thought about writing novels, I had never finished one (my

2

record was 10 chapters in, or about 23,000 words, before I scrapped the whole thing). And then I just began writing a book and I kept writing it. And it got up to 50,000 words and my parents pressured me into submitting what I had to this writing camp in our area.

The writing camp—Lindrick Camp for Young Authors, Poets, and Writers—was located in the middle of the forest. It was only open to high school kids. Each summer, kids would go there and collaborate with other writers to become better writers and to network with each other so they could help each other out in the future. And it was good for brainstorming. And it was good for just being in a space where everybody understood you because they were *like* you.

I didn't really want to go though. I never had any interest in going to a summer camp. I liked the solitude of my room in the summer. The quiet, sleepy meadows behind my house. The distant sounds of the toll highway that had been built just a few years prior. I liked it at home. But my parents insisted I submit an application.

So I did.

And to nobody's surprise but my own, I actually got into the damn place. They offered me a spot and my parents refused to let me refuse the offer. The book I had entered was about two kids that get stuck in a mall during a blizzard. It's called {*23:59*}, if you cared.

My friends were excited, even though it meant I wouldn't get to see them for a long while. Our summer vacation starts June 27 and ends on September 5. That's 70 days. The camp starts on June 30, a Saturday, and ends on September 2, a Sunday, and that adds up to 65 days. Leaving just 5 days for me and my friends to hang out before school starts again.

The only benefits about this writing camp are these: 1) I get to write freely because that's literally all I'm there to do, and 2) the camp has mandatory writing classes and workshops and lectures and seminars through the summer and these things combined add up to one full English credit, meaning I get an extra free period next year instead of having to sit in a dull English class listening to an old man or woman drone on about Shakespeare or T. S. Eliot. And if I remember the packet correctly, it also grants us an elective credit, meaning we could take another free period if we so wished.

But anyway, that brings us to the day I packed...

My backpack was bulging. I had a several empty notebooks and my MacBook inside of it. I did all my novel writing on the MacBook, but I wrote poems, random thoughts, and drawings (correction: scribbly sketches) in the notebooks. I had another bag—strictly for clothing—sitting on my bed, full to the brim with clothes. Socks, jeans, underwear, and T-shirts. That's all I ever wore. My style was simple because simple never drew attention.

"Dalton!" my mom yelled up to me. "We have to leave soon. Are you gonna be ready or what?" I could tell by the tone in her voice that she was excited about this, more so than I was. It was just like going to school, except not at all like that. I guess I just didn't see how much writing camp would alter the course of my life. (But hindsight is 20/20 as they say.)

"Yeah!" I shouted back to her. "I'll be ready in a few." I sighed and shut my luggage bag, the one with my clothes. I took a look around my room. It was always weird seeing my room that one last time before leaving to go somewhere. Maybe I'm just a sap, or maybe I just always liked the nostalgic feeling it gave me. It's like saying goodbye to a friend knowing that you will, in fact, see each other again someday.

I zipped up my backpack. I did a mental double-check to make sure I didn't forget shampoo or deodorant. (There's a store on-camp, but I wanted to be prepared). I zipped up my luggage and dropped it to the ground.

I walked to the bathroom to go pee. It's a pretty far drive

to this camp so I wanted to pee. I peed. I then washed my hands and looked at my face in the mirror. My defining quality had always (and will always be) my stark green eyes and my jet-black hair. Other than that, I'm pretty average. I don't have a striking jawline or a beautiful smile or a fancy haircut or anything like that. Just an average dude with dark hair and bright eyes that looks like he barely gets any sleep. *Aesthetic.*

I gave my teeth a quick brushing and rinsed my mouth with mouthwash before picking up my backpack, swinging it on my back, and then heading up the stairs with my luggage bag being dragged behind me. I bet my mom appreciated hearing every single *THUD* of the luggage bag on each step as I clamoured my way to the main floor.

"Lift," my stepdad teased as I made my way into the kitchen.

"But if I did that, how would everybody know that I disapproved of having to go to this stupid camp?" I asked. In the world of clichés, this was a popular one. The stroppy teenager going away to camp or a vacation thing. It's played out, but it's accurate. I didn't want to go to camp, and I didn't care how clichéd that made me.

"Come on, you'll have fun," my mom said, entering the kitchen from the living room. She smiled at me. "You will. Just give it a chance to be fun."

I scoffed. "You're right. My idea of fun is sitting around with a bunch of strangers, getting eaten alive by mosquitos, and taking turns doing dishes."

"That's not *all* camp is about," my sister, Liza, chimed in from her spot sitting on the stairs leading upstairs. I figured that she would come for the ride, but sometimes I would have believed that she had better things to do with her time.

"Because you've been to *this* camp?" I asked, rhetorically in theory.

"No, but my friend was at a band camp last year. She had a lot of fun." Liza's friend probably did have fun, and I would have fun too, if I were more like Liza's friend, but I am

5

not, I am me, and that's who I had always been, and who I will always be. I'm not ashamed of me. I just didn't like to being around people all the time, with the exception of my friends and my girlfriend (when I have one). I decided not to answer Liza's comment. No point.

My stepdad took my luggage back and went outside to load it into the SUV. I heard the engine rumble to life. The time was nearing for me to say goodbye for the summer to my home. I had already said goodbye yesterday to my friends. I promised to message them (pending how good the service is at camp) and that I'd see them the first day I was back home.

And so it began.

TWO

Though I've never enjoyed it, I could see why people gravitated towards Northern Ontario. There's nothing here. *Nothing.* There's no big cities, just small little suburban towns and cottages. Everything is a million times more serene than even in a town like Belleville, and Belleville isn't all that big itself. But there's such a drop-off. There's less cars. The roads open up and you get to drive faster. The buildings and houses fade away and thickets of trees and rivers and creeks begin to swallow everything you see.

Northern Ontario, and by that I meant everything north of Lake Ontario, basically, is a forest. Once you're a few kilometres up from the shore, that's all it is. And lakes. Oh, my goodness, were there ever lakes! And these were those beautiful, picturesque, postcard-perfect lakes. The ones with flocks of loons and geese and ducks. The ones that were so clear and undisturbed that the sky reflected back at you like a perfect mirror.

But there's downsides to the forest. Deerflies and black flies and horseflies and pretty much every other small, buzzing, winged thing with small jaws for biting lived in forests of Ontario. Effectively meaning that if you want to have fun in the woods, you would have to take a Frontenac shower (which is the name we kids in the city gave to using liberal amounts of bug spray).

Watching the trees whiz by the SUV (or us whiz by the trees) took my mind to other places. I didn't so much focus on where we going, but rather, I just got lost in daydreaming. Fantasies about how great camp would really be. Daydreaming that I would win a prestigious award for writing and get an instant book deal and make millions on a movie deal and become a best-selling phenomenon over the summer. It's nice to have dreams. I've always thought it keeps you grounded knowing that dreams are dreams. My goal was to finish writing the novel I had been working on though. That was probably the one good thing I looked forward to. Hell, with all the free time, I could probably end up writing a new book or two.

The drive took a little longer than I would have liked. We passed by the street we needed to turn down, but then we decided to stop for lunch at a café just north of the camp in Sharbot Lake, a little blink-and-you-miss-it town located on, well, Sharbot Lake. It's a nice town. Not much to see or do though. It mostly exists to remind people driving through that other people still exist, despite the density of trees and lack of anything else.

The café is also small. But what else would anyone expect from a small town. It's in a building that vaguely resembles what could have once been a town church. I spent my coffee and bagel thinking about what the camp looks like. I hadn't seen it in person or even in pictures. I never wanted to. All I had seen up to this point was the picture of the front sign, the sign you see at the end of their long dirt road of a driveway:

Lindrick Camp for Young Authors, Poets, & Writers. It sounded as pretentious as I had always thought a camp for young authors, poets, and writers could sound. The sign was wooden with metal letters bolted on. There was a small archway above that said something in Latin, something like: "Creativitas liberabit vos" written in all capital letters between the two thin curved poles of the archway. It was every bit as pretentious as you're imagining it. And I get the irony. I'm pretentious too.

Liza snaps me out of my daydreaming about how shit this camp will be when she drops her fork on the floor. She's well finished her poutine by now, so it's not like she needs it to eat, but the sound was enough to snap me back into the conversation my family was having. They were talking amongst themselves about how nice it is in this town. I guess none of them have ever been up this way. I was here before with my grandpa. He took me fishing out on one of the million lakes in this part of Ontario. So I let myself drown their conversation out as I took my phone from my pocket and checked Facebook. My friends had messaged me to tell me to let them know when I got there and then again when I got settled in.

They were taking bets on if I would have to sit through a boring welcome assembly or not. Smart money would be that, yes, I would have to sit through a boring welcome assembly. That's how the world works.

The dirt road leading to the camp was barely a car's width across. Just this narrow strip of dirt going in and out. There were little wide spots along the road that you could pull into so other cars could pass, but it'd still be a tight fit. And then, without warning, the dirt road opened up to a large dirt patch. And on this patch of dirt sat several cars, trucks, and vans. And there were several kids milling about with parents and bags in tow.

"I guess we're in the right place," my mom said as the SUV pulled into a de facto parking spot. My stepdad turned the key and the SUV shut off.

"Doesn't look so bad," Liza said. I still wondered why she bothered to come. She's not a writer, so she can't be scouting this place out for her to spend a future summer here. But then again, she's only 14, so perhaps she wants to take up writing. I'd feel honoured for her to follow in her big bro's footsteps, to be honest.

And perhaps the summer wouldn't be *terrible*. Aside from all the small, flying things that want to bite me and suck my blood, the temperatures never get very hot. The hottest they usually got was maybe 23°C. That's very mild, very enjoyable. And with the trees everywhere, shade was in abundance, so sunburns were out of the question (mostly). I had made sure to pack sweaters, just in case I was ever out at night. The nights in the forest can get pretty cold, so you've gotta be prepared for that. I had managed to get a sweater, three jeans, a bunch of socks, seven T-shirts, and a set of pyjamas into my luggage bag. So I was set for the summer, granted I remember to laundry frequently.

I got out of the SUV and opened the trunk. I pulled the handle of my luggage and the bag rolled onto the dirt (a foot drop at least) with a *THUD*, sending dust up at my shins. I suppose it hadn't rained here in a few days. Maybe it would in the coming days.

I looked out to the group of people walking up to the office building of the camp. *Registration,* I thought to myself. My least favourite word. I had to get my room assignment though. As me and my mom walked up to the office, I was thinking about how the room would look. I remember having to fill out a small questionnaire about my writing habits. Maybe they'd give me the room best suited to my needs. (A wooden desk, a lamp, and a window with a screen so I can keep it open without worrying about anything flying in.)

"Hello," a young woman said. She had a nametag on her

olive drab camp counsellor shirt. Amanda, it read.

"Hello. I'm here to drop off my son," my mom said as we stepped up to the counter of the office. None of the other campers were in the office. Good. I didn't want to make awkward small talk while our parents filled out paperwork saying that they dropped us off and double-checked our files to make sure all emergency contact numbers were up to date.

The moments ticked by and I stood there with my backpack on my back and the luggage bag at my feet, handle still fully extended so I could turn and go as soon as my mom was done. She turned to me and handed me and some pieces of paper and a key. "This is your locker key and this is your room number, and there's a map here on this sheet."

I took the papers and key. "I'm okay to walk there myself," I told her.

She nodded. "Right." We walked back outside and now my stepdad and Liza were standing there waiting for us. "So this is where we leave Dalton."

And then we said our goodbyes, which I will spare retelling about because it was just a goodbye to family. I watched the trio go back to the SUV and get in. And then I watched the SUV drive down the dusty road back towards home. A younger me would have ran after them. A younger me would be crying about being left alone, but there are other kids around, and I would have to be strong regardless.

I turned and started off toward the central camp facilities. There were a few buildings. The office was in the front, there was a cafeteria and kitchen building on the right side of the little central square. Or so the map said. The campgrounds also stretched back into a large field for football, soccer, and baseball. The map showed a pond surrounded by trees in the centre of that large field. I could also see a dirt path leading from the centre square of the camp all the way to the beach. On the opposite side of the square was a large building. It housed the common areas and dorm rooms. The boys and girls were separated by the common areas. Boys on one side and girls on the other. The common area was monitored by the occasional night patrol counsellor passing through. These map has a lot of information printed on it. The computer lab is in the dorm buildings as well.

I followed the mapped path to the dorm buildings. I looked at some of the other papers as I walked. There was a first-day timetable. We had until one o'clock to unpack and get settled in our rooms. And then at one thirty we have to go to the auditorium, which wasn't on the map because it was actually outside in that large field. I could see from here that there was a stage and a bunch of foldable metal chairs set up in front of it. The whole day from there was orientation, getting acclimatized to the camp.

My room was at the far end of the hallway. Room 41. And I noticed that all the rooms in the boys' section were odd-numbered, so logic would serve that the girls' section was even numbers. The room itself was pretty small. Only one bed, so I didn't have any roommates. The door didn't seem to have very good locks (I guess in case of emergency and they needed access?), and on the paper it mentioned that we weren't allowed visitors in our rooms unless the door was wide open and the dorm supervisor knew about it. I guess no summer blow jobs in this dorm room. What a bummer.

But it's also not like I was in the business to get blow jobs this summer. I was in the business of writing all summer long, locked in this dorm room, looking out to the field and seeing the other kids writing in their notebooks. I would just do the same things that I did in regular school. Listen, learn, and use that as a tool to make my writing better. I'm not here to make friends with people who live in Smiths Falls or Ottawa or Brighton or even Belleville. I'm here to write.

I shut the door (as I'm allowed so long as I am alone) and sat on the bed. The sheets were new, soft, and they smelt like lavender laundry detergent. In the corner by the window sat a small wooden desk. There was a black chair sitting there as well. I guess they had tailored my room to me a little bit, or maybe my needs were just standard issue.

I unpacked a little bit, killing an hour just figuring out how to log into the Wi-Fi network. It wasn't very fast, but it was fast enough to be able to scroll Facebook and send messages home to friends and family. So I did just that. I messaged my friends to let them know I was safely at the camp and settling into my room. I also told them I won the bet about orientation. I don't know why any of them would bet on fun orientation or no orientation. Or maybe they knew I needed a quick little cheer-me-up, and winning a bet always did the trick.

THREE

The sun was bright in the sky, hanging up there in the vast pale blueness. I wondered sometimes about how lonely the sun must feel. Probably not at all, because it's a star and stars don't have feelings. Though some might, and we might not ever know. I craned my neck back to Earth level and focused on tying my shoes. They had come undone in the time it took for me to walk from my dorm room to the camp square (the grassy area with a few trees in the middle of all the buildings and bordered by the large open field).

I followed the semi-formed group of other campers (I guess that's what I'll call them) to the field. The "auditorium" was actually a lot larger than I thought. The stage was up higher and was deeper and wider than what it had seemed at first. There was a lonely microphone sitting there, and some speakers on either side. There were maybe 60 chairs set up. Six rows of ten chairs, spaced out down the centre from the stage.

On my way to the seats, I noticed a girl sitting in the grass. She was plucking at a small garden of dandelions. She pulled them out of the earth, popped the tops of them off, and tied a not in the stem before tossing the stem aside as well. She looked frail, like a flower, like a dandelion. Her olive skin was yellowed on her fingers from the dandelions and green and brown on her legs from where the ground at made contact with her. She was wearing a short sundress, a white one with a flowery print on it. Her long brown hair flowed down her shoulders and back, and it flowed with the wind or when she would flick her head to move it herself. I watched her for long enough to know that one strand of her hair kept falling into her face. And that's when I realized I needed to keep moving, because I was really stretching the amount of time one person should be ogling at another.

I made my way to a seat in the last row. The idea of being attacked by a lost bear was more appealing than being in a row where strangers behind me could judge me from the back of my head or the way I sat in the chair, and what if my butt crack were to be at all visible? I didn't need that negativity in my life.

So I took my seat. I was one of the first kids there, and the other kids were sitting in small groups of three or four and were chatting amongst themselves, no doubt friends from last summer or from their respective hometowns. I watched them comingle. They came in all different sizes. Tall, short, stocky, lanky, chubby. Boys and girls. Not a huge diversity of skin colour though, because this part of Ontario is like 90% European descent. (There are some towns that have a 96% white demographic. It's actually really bizarre.) They all sat at the front, leaving me sitting alone at the back of a small sea of black chairs.

More kids came to the chairs. I checked my phone for the time. We still had a good fifteen minutes before the start of whatever speech the camp director would undoubtedly give us. And so more kids piled in. Soon enough, the camp counsellors and teachers made their way to the seats as well. There wasn't a pattern I could detect for how they sat. They just sat wherever, talking amongst themselves as well as some of the kids.

I watched the crowd for the girl I had seen with the dandelions. She wasn't around yet. I looked back to where she should have been still sitting on the grass, but she wasn't there either. I wondered what she was here for. Was she a novelist? A poet? A comic book artist? I remember her slender fingers popping the heads off the dandelions and thought, *Poet, for sure.* She just had that aura about her.

She looked like a poem come to life.

She looked like beauty if it had a human persona.

She looked like the universe called her home.

And I was lost deep in thought by the time the microphone crackled with a small bout of feedback. I shook out the stars and looked around. I saw her sitting a seats down from me in the next row up. I could see her swinging her leg back and forth, dangling a shoe from her bare feet. She was holding a dandelion in her fingers, absent-mindedly plucking the little tiny petals from it, one by one, as she stared towards the stage. She was nodding every so often. I could see the girl next to her talking a mile a minute. She laughed. The girl next to her laughed too. *Friends,* I thought. The friend was a petite girl with light brown hair.

They were both beautiful. In their own ways, they were both constellations in the night sky. I wondered if they met here, or if they've always been friends, or if they just met ten minutes ago and their personalities clicked so well in that first ten minutes that they're now official best friends for the summer.

I dunno. I wasn't here to make friends, but making friends is sort of nice. So maybe I was a little envious of all these kids and their friends. I could see that I was one of the only loner kids here, one of the only newbies. I could see another guy sitting alone. And a girl at the other end of the back row, like me, sitting alone and not talking to anybody.

And then a man in a brown suit walked onto the stage and cleared his throat. He had greying brown hair. Fitting for a camp director, I suppose. And he began to speak.

"Hello, writers and teachers, campers and counsellors." His voice was gruff. He must do a lot of speaking. "I am Mr. Lindrick, the camp director. Most of you know that, but there are a few new campers this summer."

And that's where he lost me. Instead of paying attention, I found my eyes fixated on the clouds rolling through the sky above. Mr. Lindrick just droned on and on about the basics of the camp, the rules, the class times, the everything. The gist was that each writing "speciality" (poetry, novels, comics, etc.) would have specialized morning classes, we'd break for lunch and then have collaborative writing, which is a fancy way of saying we would have classes with people from other circles of writing to see how their writing processes and styles were different from our own, but in a classroom. The afternoon classes also covered creative writing as a whole and the history of writing and printing presses and et cetera. I suppose the history of prose has its place in modern prose as well.

"...and with that said, I hope you all enjoy your time here." And he departed the stage. I had managed to make it through the gruelling two hours of speeches, rules, lectures, class overviews, and all that other shit. There were brochures and books and papers in my room that had all the information on it already, but I suppose some people like being *told* about things rather than just reading it themselves.

I waited to get up for a few moments. I let everybody else pile out of the field and towards their dorms where they would still be unpacking most likely. I was still trying to figure out how to make my room *mine* too.

Once the auditorium was empty, I got up. I watched the last of the kids and counsellors making their way back to the centre square. I walked to where that girl had been sitting.

She had left the dandelion on the ground in front of her chair. So I picked it up. She had plucked the petals off of half of it. I took a seat in her chair and plucked away at the rest of the dandelion's petals until it was gone and all the yellow littered the grass at my feet.

I tied a knot in the stem like she had been doing before. I dropped it on the seat of the chair and headed back into my room. Most of the kids were inside their dorms now as well. A few of them were sitting at picnic tables in the square, talking amongst themselves, still only in groups of three.

I walked back into my room, picking a dandelion up from the small grass patch in front of the dorm room first though. In my room, I plucked away at the feathers and left them sprinkled on my desk. I had my door closed as well. I didn't want anybody seeing me plucking petals from a dandelion. They might think it's weird that I was doing the same thing as that girl. Once finished, I tied a knot in the stem and put it all in my little trash can.

I guess I could have just admitted it to myself earlier, but I had a crush on this girl that I hadn't spoken to yet. She was just so beautiful. And seeing her made me realize why people wrote loves songs about people they barely know.

My room came together nicely. I had stuck up a few small posters that I brought, just to liven the place a little, make it feel just a bit more like home. I spent a while going through all those papers too, and just to reiterate: this camp voids the need to take next year's English class. And that's really all I cared about. It was an extra free period for me.

And I guess camp wasn't so bad, right? I get to just write, and write, and write. And I get to write even more after that. I had an entire summer devoted to writing (depending on if I get writer's block or not).

But this would also be one of the loneliest summers of my

life. I couldn't just go down the street and see my friends. I could hang out with my lady friend and fool around like we did sometimes when we had time off of school. (We're both horny teenagers that are scared of commitment, friends with benefits just made sense to us.) And I couldn't see my mom or stepdad or sister because they're all an hour and a half away, back in Belleville. And that's saddening. I was alone here, but not *alone*, but lonely enough to feel alone. Despite what most people think, you can feel like you're on the surface of Mars even though you're in a room full of people.

And this summer, I was a Martian.

FOUR

The first "free" day of camp was the following day, the Sunday. It was sunny like yesterday had been, but still not very hot, despite it being now July. Which reminds me, today is Canada Day, which is weird for me to be spending it at camp like this. I usually go to the lakeshore and watch fireworks. I heard they would do fireworks at camp too, and that Monday would be a free day as well to account for the civic holiday. Classes started Tuesday.

I wasn't, however, ready to be a part of a crowd for the fireworks tonight. Canada Day fireworks were a staple of Canadian student summer vacations. It was the night that *really* kicked off the summer vacation. A whole two months of sunshine, riding bikes, and hanging out in our friends' basements.

But nope. Not this year. I would be getting grass stains on my ass and hands as I sat on the field and looked upwards to the sparkling night sky. And the fireworks would shoot up, whizzing into the air and then going quiet before a loud *POP* and then a starburst of bright light.

I got lost in it, actually. The lights of the fireworks. I got lost enough not to notice the dandelion girl or the fact I spilt my cup of water or that my legs were going numb from the way I had been sitting on them.

I just got lost. In the lights and sounds. Every whiz longer than the last. Every burst of light more colourful than those that came before. And every loud bang rattled my bones and left me wanting another one and another one until it was over. And the fireworks stopped and the moon hung by a thread in the sky and we all went back to our dorms and we fell asleep. And I sat at my desk with my MacBook open on a low brightness.

And I picked apart a dandelion I had brought back to my room from the field, littering my desk and keyboard with tiny yellow petals.

Sometimes, I wondered about if other people viewed people in the same ways I did. Like, if someone else though that X person had a nice smile or that Y person was too tall for their frame or whatever it was.

I wondered what they thought of me too. How could I not? I spent my life being alone, and so I wondered what people thought of that. Of the kid just sitting there, doodling in his notebook, and writing nonsense until sense was made.

On the Monday, our first free day of the summer, technically, I was sat on a bench, writing in my notebook. One of several that I had brought to camp with me. I was just absent-mindedly writing in my notebook, enjoying the sunshine, and not bothering anybody. I watched several kids walk by to go to the beach or to the baseball diamond or to kick a soccer ball around the soccer pitch, but not for me. I was here to write, and write I did.

I watched the dandelion girl and her friend as they walked to the field. Her friend left after a few minutes. Dandelion girl was wearing a thick tuque, even though it was 22°C in the sun and the humidity made it feel more like 27°C, she was still in the hat, and a black one at that. I wondered if I could ever actually speak to her. It's not like I was a friend of her friend. I was just a stranger. And a girl that beautiful probably has a boyfriend. But I needed to be more open with other writers. And maybe she'd just be a great friend to me. Not every pretty person has to be a mate, I guess, right? Boys and girls can be friends without the underlying notion that at some point they have to catch feelings for one another.

And it makes sense to talk to her from the writing aspect. It's a writing camp. We're all writers here, in some way or another.

And I promise she's not just a manic pixie dream girl. She's not going to save me and she's not the only girl I noticed. I noticed other people. The boy with a scar on his left arm that looked like it was from a burn. There was a girl who had her hair in the tightest bun I had ever seen in my life. I didn't *just* notice dandelion girl. But this story is about her as much as it is me, because on this Monday, I got up and walked over to where she was sitting in the field, and I opened my mouth to talk to her.

"Isn't it hot with that hat on?" I asked her.

She looked up from her notebook at me. She was even more beautiful up close. Her eyes shone amber in the sunlight. And then she squinted to get a fix on me. And she spoke, "It's a very cozy hat." Her voice was honey. It was sunshine. It was the auditory equivalent of a warm blanket.

I smiled softly. "May I sit?"

She nodded and buried her eyes back to the notebook. I sat next to her. The grass was still cool and refreshing despite it being out in the sun for the morning. "This place," she said, "is a nice place to relax."

I could see in her fingertips that she had been popping the heads off of more dandelions from the neon yellow that had stained them. She had a ring on her index finger and another one on the opposite hand's pinky finger. I nodded slowly. "Yeah. I've never been here before. I'm new this summer."

"I can tell," she said softly, not like she meant it venomously, but it sounded somewhat conceited, as if she were telling me that she knew everything that goes on here before the rest of us do. Just that tone of voice. I then wondered if maybe this girl was a bitch. Just because someone is beautiful doesn't mean they're a *good* person. You can be a beautiful asshole or a beautiful sweetheart or an ugly saint. There's no law about these things. Maybe this beautiful and delicate-looking girl was just a bitch. Or maybe she's having a bad day. Or maybe I'm just intruding on alone time she wanted and she's too nice or shy to ask me to go away.

I opened my notebook and read over what I had written earlier. Not much of anything good. Just bouncing ideas around in my mind about my book. I closed it and looked at the dandelion girl. She was furiously writing in her notebook, not even paying attention that I was sitting beside her, much less that I was trying to have a conversation.

"So, are you a poet or a novelist?" I asked her. She looked over at me and stared daggers into my soul. It was enough of a cutting stare that I felt the air leave my lungs for a moment. How could such a cute face look so angry?

Her nose flared a little and she furrowed her brow. "Don't you know that it's rude to intrude on other people's writing time? Do I bother you when you're scribbling in your little notebook?" She said it like having a notebook was a demonizing thing even though she had one too. "You shouldn't just barge into other people's creative space like that. I'll see you in class. We can talk then or some other time, but for now I'd like to write in silence and solitude, please and thank you."

I nodded and chewed my cheek. "Of course," I said, getting up. "Sorry to bother you. See you around."

I walked away. I walked fast. I walked with purpose. I wanted to put as much distance as I could between us. I had just botched that. Fuck. First impressions mean so much and I just fucked up. Whatever. There's other girls here. Other girls back home. Countless other people to be friends with too. And so what if I screwed that up. At least I talked to someone new. I tried. And that's the more important thing, that I tried, not so much that the outcome wasn't positive for my end.

I found myself sitting on a bench near the baseball diamond. The sun was still beating down on the field, but it wasn't very hot. Though my cheeks were still flush from the embarrassment of that painful interaction with the dandelion girl.

My ass started to hurt from the wooden bench, so I moved to the grass, next to a small patch of dandelions, and I pulled some out and set them down in front of me. I popped the heads off of them and tied knots in the stems. It was around then that I noticed the two guys tossing a baseball back and forth in the baseball diamond.

I kept writing and wondered what I could have said differently to that girl. I didn't even get her name. And I didn't even get to give her mine. I supposed that didn't really matter now. She had barely looked at me. She only looked up at me when I came over, so I must have looked like a shadow to her. Maybe if I spoke with a different accent and tried again tomorrow, she wouldn't even know it was me.

But that'd be tomorrow and today was still today and I was still sitting in this stupid field, writing in my notebook, wishing I had said pretty much *anything* else to *anyone* else.

FIVE

Everything was uncomfortable. My relishing in a botched conversation, my sitting in this field in the sun. I hadn't even brought sunscreen, so in all likelihood, my poor pale skin would be red as tomatoes by the end of the week and as dark as coffee with a dash of cream by the end of the summer. I'll go home looking far different at least.

The sun wasn't terribly hot or bright and there was an abundance of shaded areas, I supposed my level of sunburtness depended on how much time I spent out in the direct sunlight. But as I sat in the field, I let the sun cook me.

For instance, I had wished I remembered to bring a pair of earphones out to the field too. Though the distant sounds of two kids playing catch was calming in a way, and the sounds of other people occasionally shouting in the distance was also a little calming. And the sound of the wind and the chirping of birds as they fluttered overhead. At least my loneliness was calming today.

I found myself doodling in the notebook however. Writing words down.

She's busy doing nothing, but she's busy killing time.
Lies awake every night, can never get any sleep.
"Dammit," she breaths, "How will I ever find my place?"

I'm not sure what it meant. Just random little thoughts I've had. I thought they were poetic, but I guess they're more pathetic.

And see, my friends are living life and getting jobbed up.
And I'm still thinking 'bout the past and feeling fucked up.

More nonsense, really.

The stars look down on us and wonder,
"How could one person mean so much to another?"

My rereading is broken by the sound of nearing footsteps. I close my notebook and look up to see one of the two kids who were playing catch walking up to me. "Why so glum, bud?" he asked, his stereotypical Canadian accent very noticeable.

"Just writing," I told him.

He didn't buy it. "Come on. You can tell me. I'm your friend." He stuck his hand out to me. "Taron Smith. The other one is Seth." Taron is a stout ginger boy. He has more freckles on his face than the night sky has stars. But somehow, it still didn't seem like enough. Seth is taller. He has dark hair and thick-rimmed glasses, hipster style glasses though, not nerd style.

I take his hand and he helps me to my feet. "I just tried talking to that girl over there." I answered his question as I pointed over towards the dandelion girl.

Taron cracked a smile and laughed softly. "Jasmine," he

said, "was not a good choice for you to open with. She hates being bothered when she goes out to write. If you see a notebook in her hands, it's best to leave her alone, *unless* you're her best friend, boyfriend, brother, mom, dad, or if she offers you to tag along with her, which is rare."

"Oh. She seems serious about her notebook."

Taron nodded. "She's been working on a super-secret poetry project. She's been working on it every summer, and only in the summers, for the past two years."

"How old is she?" I asked, desperate for more information.

"Sixteen, just like Seth and I." Taron looked me over. It could be that my face hasn't gotten the chiseling of definition from puberty yet, because he then said, "And I would assume you're, what, fourteen?"

"Sixteen," I corrected. "How do you know so much about her?"

"I used to be her friend." Taron grinned. "Anyway, enough about Jasmine. You're here with us now," he told me. "You're new this summer, right?"

I nodded. "I didn't want to come, actually. My parents just thought it would be good to meet with other young writers. I didn't even know this kind of place existed up until a couple months ago." I began following Taron over to the baseball diamond.

"Yeah," Taron began, "this place is pretty fucking sweet. This is my third summer here. I'm a comic writer and artist. I found this place online one night and begged my parents for months to pay for my application, and then I got in and never looked back." He turned to Seth. "Seth, this is—" He turned to me and gave me a blank look.

"Dalton," I told them.

"My boy Dee," Seth said with a wide grin. I guess Dee is easier to say than Dalton. I didn't mind it though.

"He just got shot down by Jasmine," Taron informed Seth.

Seth gave me a slight look of pity. "She's always reclusive in the first week. Don't take it personally. She'll lighten up. What'd you say to her?"

"I just asked if she was a poet or a novelist."

"Poet," Taron told me.

"And a bitchy one at that," Seth muttered. "Anyway, what are you?"

"Novelist, I suppose," I told them.

Taron sighed and Seth smiled approvingly. "We had a bet going."

"Yeah," Taron began, "every novelist or short story writer that comes, I have to give this idiot five bucks, and every new anything else, he gives me five bucks. That other new girl, Terri, she writes short stories, mostly about animals that can talk."

"They're actually quite good," Seth added. "I scoped her Wattpad page last night."

"How do you know her Wattpad?" I questioned.

He smirked. "Because we asked her, smarty-pants."

"Yeah. We like taking an interest in the people here. It's either we read what they've written or we stare at the walls all night," Taron added. "And, to be fair, I actually really like reading their stuff."

"There was one girl here last summer that wrote poetry exclusively about vegetables and fruits," Seth stated. "She was vegan."

"But the poetry was surprisingly moving," Taron said.

And they both poeticized, "Green like my eyes, the cucumber on my plate / red like the sky, a cutting sun, my tomato / lettuce leaf, smells catch the breeze / a summer salad for you and for me."

"Not all of them were good," Taron told me. "But we liked that one. She called it *Summer Salad*."

"I can see why," I said.

"Some people find their niche early on and just ride with it," Seth stated. "For instance, Taron makes comics for a target audience of only himself."

"Fuck off, bud." I could tell that these two were pretty close friends. I wondered if perhaps they were from the same town and just happened to recognize each other at camp. They sure seemed to be the best of buds. (I guess because you'd have to be best friends with someone to just toss a ball back and forth for an hour like they had been doing before I so rudely interrupted with my silent writing.)

"So, Dee, where are you from?" Seth asked.

"Belleville," I told him.

"Smiths Falls, myself. Taron's from the great big city of Ottawa," Seth replied. Okay, so I guess they weren't from the same town, but I'd still place strong money on them spending a lot of time playing online video games with each other while bouncing their ideas off one another. Seth tossed the ball to Taron. "So, Dee, did you wanna throw this ball around with us for a bit? I've got more gloves in my bag." Seth nodded towards a large black duffel bag on the ground.

I nodded. I wasn't the best at throwing things, but I figured I should at least try to extend the politeness. They had talked to me and given me information, and for a brief moment, made me feel like I was one of them, someone who maybe belonged here. Accepted. And with the summer sun beating down on the green field and dusty diamond, we tossed the ball back and forth, and I listened to Seth and Taron talk about nothing and everything and then more nothing and I didn't speak much, but I didn't need to, and they didn't force me to or ask why I didn't. They accepted me as I was.

SIX

In hindsight, I should have seen it coming. The first night before classes and camp officially "started" in the literal sense. There's always a prank to the new kids. Just how there's usually an end-of-the-summer prank, thought the pranks on new kids are obviously a lot smaller in scale and a lot more individual.

That brings me back to the first morning of classes, when I, a new camper, was placed on the prank radar. I should have honestly been more prepared for something to happen. I should have padlocked my door sevenfold, just to be sure.

I woke up and my room seemed pretty undisturbed. Maybe I had gotten off light. I turned my alarm off and rubbed the sleep from my eyes. I remembered to shower last night so I wouldn't risk being pranked if I showered in the morning.

I even hid my shoes between my headboard and mattress so they couldn't steal them or the laces or put shaving cream in it or whatever genius prank they'd have come up with. I really thought I covered all my bases, but to do that, I would have had to stay up all night in vigilant alertness to thwart any and all prank attempts (which in itself would have been a prank on myself). But I needed sleep for the first day of classes. So I slept.

Anyway.

My room was dark and the morning light filtered through the trees and my window and fell in a sharp square on the floor. It lit the room up well enough though. I didn't need a light to get ready in the mornings, which was nice because saving electricity helps save the world. *One unlit morning at a time*, I thought to myself.

The air was cold. I had left the window cracked open, so I shut it and quickly looked for a shirt. But that's when I realized what the prank had been. I couldn't find a shirt. Or socks. Or a sweater. Or pants. Or even underwear. I only had the clothes I was wearing: a pair of pyjama pants and my underwear.

I grabbed my shoes from between the mattress and headboard and slid them on. Wearing shoes without socks is such a weird feeling. I looked outside, thinking maybe they had put my clothes just outside, but I couldn't see anything resembling clothes or a bag of clothes or anything. I looked around my room and saw a small slip of paper taped to the inside of my door. I went over and quietly read the note aloud to myself, "In a bag in the square, you should find your clothes there." I sighed and muttered, "Written by a poet, no doubt."

So I folded the paper up and put it on my desk. I walked outside like the proud kid I was, not ashamed of my slightly paler-than-the-rest-of-me chest. I didn't eat like shit and I routinely go to the gym once in a while, so I was in decent shape. I felt somewhat confident, is what I guess I'm trying to say.

I stepped outside into the day and the sun hits my face

and chest, radiating its warmth to me from millions of miles away. I smile softly to myself and looked around the square as I stepped down the little wooden steps of the dorm building. I couldn't see anything in the trees, so I knew it was gonna be a little bit of a search. There was a dozen or so trees in the square to make it well shaded enough to make it a viable hangout area.

A girl caught my eye. I turned to get a better look and watched as Terri tried to climb up a tree to retrieve her clothes. I guess she had been pranked as well. I wondered where the other new kids were, but maybe they already got their clothes back, or maybe they're still asleep, or maybe they got pranked differently.

I also saw Jasmine sitting at a bench with that one girl that's clearly her friend. She made eye contact with me and low-key giggled at seeing me in my sleeping attire out in the daylight. Maybe making a snide remark about my paleness or the shape and size of my nipples. Teenagers make comments about dumb things sometimes.

I shrugged it off and started looking for my clothes. In a bag, the note had told me. I looked around until I saw a bright orange bag in a tree. It was pretty high up there. I looked back to Terri and she was only in the first section of branches getting her bag. Mine was a lot higher. I wonder why. I wonder who climbed that high in the middle of the night. I wondered how I didn't hear anybody rifling through my closet. It's not like I wear earplugs to bed.

I looked the tree over and tried to devise the quickest and safest route to the top to get my bag. And usually safe and quick are not the same route. Anyway, I took a running jump up to the tree and pulled myself into the thicket of branches at the lower level. My hands found their grip quickly on the next branch, and the next one, and the next one, and I just moved upwards, staying firmly focused on the orange bag. This was also a way to prove to everybody that I won't say no to a challenge.

I reached the top of the tree and poked my head out above the shrubbery. The wind was nice, nothing in the way to obstruct its flow as it moved in around me. I felt it on my cheeks, warm and cooling at the same time. I looked over the field and the rest of the camp. I was just up over roof level. The highest spot you could get to, I suppose, without going into the woods to climb one of the bigger trees.

I tossed the bag a few branches down. It was heavy to move, so I didn't wanna sling it on my back or just drop it to the ground. It took me a lot longer to get down than it did to get to the top. I took my time, to make sure I didn't fall. I dropped the bag from the lowest branch to the ground and then dropped down next to it. Jasmine gave me a small smile as I did. I saw Taron in the distance and he turned to me and gave me a thumbs up.

The bag was surprisingly easier to swing onto my back than I thought. I walked back into the dorms and got dressed. I had plenty of time to make it to class before the ten start time. It was only still barely nine. I collected myself and head back into the square. Jasmine and her friend were gone.

Seth was there though. And he trudged over to me. "Good morning." He held out a coffee cup to me. "It's got some cream and sugar in it."

"Thank you," I told him, taking the cup from him.

"I hear you got pranked. The classic clothes in the tree. That one happened to me too. It happens to all short story writers and novelists."

"The pranks are split up by type of literature?" I asked.

Seth nodded and took a sip of coffee. "Sure. Writers get their clothes hung in the trees. Poets get their shoes tied to a stick in the creek. The rest of them get their doorknobs greased and their eyebrow removed in their sleep. And it's okay because it usually grows back by the end of the summer."

"So Taron…"

"Yes, and I have pictures. You'll see them someday, don't

worry." Seth took a small breath and another sip of coffee. "Anyway, we have class to get to."

"You're in my class?"

"You're a writer, a novelist, a whatever. I am too. We're in the same class in the morning." He nodded his head. "Follow me. You might get lost amongst all the one building."

"So why the prank?"

Seth shrugged. "I don't know. Just something to do for fun, I guess. It helps you loosen up a little bit. Some kids just need to see that we're all here to have fun and be friends. Nobody's out to get anybody, really. I've seen some nasty kids here. They usually go home after two weeks though, so that's nice. Nobody likes a bunch of Negative Neds running around."

I took a sip of my coffee as he spoke. It was actually a very good coffee. Arabica, not Columbia. Which is good, because I don't like Columbia. "I'm trying to imagine you and Taron getting pranked. You two seem like The New Campers Guide to the Summer."

"Because we've been through the motions before. When we were new kids, these other dudes passed on their wisdom to us. One of them is actually a published writer now. The other one is still trying to sell a screenplay out in Hollywood, but he's chasing his dream and you can't fault him for that." Seth was leading me down the dirt path. I saw some other kids just ahead of us.

"What was it like when you got pranked?" I asked.

Seth shrugged. "Pretty standard. They said I did a good job at anti-pranking my room, but the room I was in didn't have a proper lock on the window, so they climbed in. Didn't wake me up though, surprisingly."

"And Jasmine?"

"Back on her, is your mind?" Seth laughed. "Yeah, she had her shoes tied over the creek. Not *in* the creek, but you had to go into the creek to get them back. She actually didn't get them for a few days as a form of protest or something to the prank, but when it rained one day, she knew she couldn't walk around in mud all day, so she got her shoes for the benefit of the cleaning staff."

"Why do non-poets and non-storywriters get the eyebrow thing? That's a lingering prank. It's not like ours where it's over as soon as we retrieve our shoes or clothes." I was genuinely curious about this.

"Because we're literature elites and they're not." Seth shrugged. "I don't actually know why, we just assume it's because comic book writers and screenplay writers have better senses of humour. You know us poets and writers are all emotionally unstable alcoholics."

"Not yet."

"*Yet.*" Seth placed a finger on his nose and nodded towards a door. "This one's ours." He stuck his arm out. "After you, Dee."

And then that was the morning. I had gotten my clothes back. Later in the day, I saw a girl with half her eyebrows. Must be one of the "others." I also sat and watched another girl trying to retrieve her shoes from the creek, but she kept getting sketched out by the nonexistent fish and the rocks moving under her feet with each step. It was entertaining to watch because she wasn't in any real trouble. She did end up getting the shoes back after fifteen minutes or so.

SEVEN

Surprisingly, or not at surprisingly at all, the first few days seemed to just fly right by my eyes. Class was interesting for the most part, not to most people, but I'm a writer, so I'm a stickler for formatting and whatnot, and so I enjoyed it. Seth kept me company for the most part, talking quietly to himself or to me about whatever writing exercise we were doing.

And that was the mornings. The afternoons were spent in silence, mostly. I had earbuds with me for this class. I figured "creative writing" would just mean everybody sitting down and working on things quietly. But since I was a novelist, I was told to write poetry or draw comics for this section of classes. Jasmine was in this class with me, so that was nice. I could absent-mindedly admire her while writing or absent-mindedly write while admiring her.

I saw her walking to and from places when I would sit in the field or toss a ball with Seth and Taron. I saw her when I walked by the square and she had big red headphones on and was deep into writing on her laptop. It seemed as though she was copying stuff from her notebook onto her computer.

And the days passed by slower then. I sat and enjoyed the summer breeze whisking through the shade of the square. And she wrote and copied and rewrote. She really was something wonderful, even from afar. I must have watched her pop the tops off of seventy-three dandelions over the first week I was at camp too.

The day eventually came when things got more exciting than just classrooms and journaling all day long. I was sitting alone in the field on Saturday. I was waiting for Seth or Taron to happen by and offer me to do something with them. I'm pretty sure they were in the common room on one of the game consoles in there. Too bright and hot for them outside.

I wrote in my notebook, trying to come up with ideas for the next chapter in my novel, or perhaps ideas for my next book altogether. The point was, I was trying to be productive. My eyes were transfixed on the words on my page.

A star in my sky,
A sliver in the night.

Pretentious. I wondered how to make it better. How I could make anything better. I went over some details for {*23:59*} after that, but my eyes reverted back to that.

A sliver in the night.

I scribbled it out and rewrote it.

A sliver in the night,
A star in my sky,
A darkness surrounds a light.

And then my eye contact with the words on my page was suddenly broken by a torn piece of notebook paper being place atop my own notebook. I looked at the handwriting. A wide-looping, scribbly cursive was all across the page. It was beautiful though. I then saw the thumb at the top of the page. It was painted with pink polish. I followed the bare arm and saw Jasmine standing over me in a beige sundress.

She smiled. "Read this and tell me what you think of it."

My eyes refused to leave hers. She was beautiful up close like this. I watched her sit down next to me and she nodded towards the page she had handed me. I still couldn't turn away. Her lips looked soft and pure, and her skin looked smooth and unwrinkled, and her smile was warm, and I was melting in the summer heat and the aura of her was enveloping me, and this was just a stupid way to feel about a girl who I barely knew.

But then I did read.

The colours of the nighttime,
Fortitudes in your eyes,
And lit up against the moon,
And then I cried a seventh tear,
The last one you'd ever wipe away.
My mind raced a thousand miles today.

And I wondered,
Who would we be if not together?
Who could we be if not together?
And should we see what tomorrow brings?
Or are we just gnomes in the gardens of kings?

"I like it," I told her.

"What do you like about it?" she asked with such a pinpoint precision in her voice that it was almost as if she had spent all night practising this exact exchange of words.

"The imagery. I picture myself in this setting of a garden at night with someone I love and they're breaking my heart because of something we can't control, like maybe they're moving away or our love is drifting apart or something and the two of us, we worry about what tomorrow will be like with or without each other."

"Very good," Jasmine said, smiling. "My name is Jasmine. And you?"

"Dalton," I stated. "But you can call me Dee. That's my new nickname for the summer."

"So, *Dee*, would you like me to tell you what *I* think about this little poem?" Her dark brown eyes were bright and she looked eager to speak what was on her mind.

I nodded. "Sure. Go ahead."

"I like to think it's about two people, in love or friends or whatever, but it's clear they care about each other very deeply. One of whom is trying to pursue their dreams as a writer or poet or actor, and the other is in school to be a nurse or a mechanic or whatever. And the artsy one is wanting to go away on pursue their dreams and so they have to break the heart of the one they love, or their friend. And so then they wonder if this is the right choice or not or if it doesn't matter because God has a plan for all of us, not that I'm religious— I'm not, I think it's a sham—but it paints a nice image, huh? That we're just gnomes in the garden of kings?"

"Yeah, I guess. I liked that line a lot."

She smiled. "I do too." She took the page back and read it over. "And should we see what tomorrow brings? / or are we just gnomes"—pause—"in the gardens of kings?" She waited for a moment for my reply.

"Perhaps we are."

She smiled at me. "You don't mind if I sit here and write, do you?" She pulled her notebook out of her bag and opened it before I could even reply.

"Go ahead. I like the company," I told her. More to the point, I liked *her* company. I watched as she dug through her bag for a pencil. She pulled a sharpener out as well and set it down on the grass as she crossed her legs over. The notebook rested on her calves and she gave the pencil a few quick twists in the sharpener to revive its point. Her legs looked so soft. The urge to run my fingertips down her shins was strong.

"It's a nice day," she said as she started doodling something at the bottom of a page in her notebook.

I nodded. "Yeah. Warm." A breeze floated through us and whisked her hair around softly, playfully almost. "So I've seen you popping the heads off of dandelions. Why do you do that?"

Jasmine shrugged. "Stress relief, I guess. Don't you do anything to relieve stress?"

I thought to myself, *Masturbate, eat, sleep, and now that I think about it, I've taken to popping heads off of dandelions as well.* But I said, "Writing is my stress relief, I guess."

"That's a good one. And I'm glad to hear you're serious about writing."

"Why?"

"Because if you weren't, then why would you be here? I mean, this is a *writing* camp for writers. So I'd hope you're serious."

I nodded. "I am."

"What do you do?" She hasn't looked up from her doodling once since she started, and that saddened me a little because I loved watching her eyes flicker around my face.

"I write novels and short stories. I'm focusing on novels now though. Short stories are played out for me."

Jasmine smiled. "That's cool. You should try poetry. I like it. It's what I do. I just write my feelings down and that's that."

"Why did you start writing poetry?"

She shrugged. "I'm a girl with a lot of emotions and I wanted to vent them. I wrote in a journal when I was younger, but I started learning bigger and fancier words, so then I made them rhyme or used evocative metaphors and then *vio-*

40

la, I was a poet and I didn't even know it."

"You can do a rhyme anytime."

"Okay, MC Novelist."

I laughed a little. "Anyway, why do you like poetry?"

"It paints pictures with words," she replied. She always speaks like she had rehearsed these lines over and over again the night before. Her voice was just so perfect in pitch, tone, and pace that it seriously sounded as though she knew every word that would be said to her before she even met the person that would say them. She turned and looked at me. "Why do you like novels?"

Shrugging, I replied, "I just like to tell stories. I like being able to transform characters over the course of a novel and telling a story, letting people imagine it as it unfolds. It's a nice feeling."

"You like to tell stories?" Her face lit up and her eyes were shimmering in the sunlight. Her lips curled up into a subtle smile.

I nodded. "I do, yes."

"Tell me a story."

"Sure." I thought for a moment. I wondered what I could tell her. I'm not good at on-the-spot stories. All my novels and short stories have planning behind them, they always will. You need to do some planning before writing or telling a story, going in blind leaves you open to a lot more plot holes and rushed endings, or maybe sometimes it drags on too long at certain parts. And so I thought. And she watched me, listening to my thoughts on the breeze.

"You don't have to tell me a long story, or even a good one. I'll be happy with any and all stories." She smiled at me, reassuring me that it did not have to be a good story, but I wanted it to be a good story, because she deserves good things, we all do once in a while. And right now, I'm saying she deserves a good story.

"Once upon a time," I began, because you have to begin every spoken story with that phrase, "there was this girl."

"Tell me about her," Jasmine said.

"She was beautiful. She had olive skin and dark chocolatey brown eyes and her lips were soft and her skin was as smooth as silk. Her voice was the most beautiful voice in the entire world, it made men fall at her feet when she said as much as 'Hello.'"

"She sounds lovely."

"She was, or is. Anyway, existing at the same time in a place not so faraway was a boy with pale skin and dark hair and bright green eyes. And, oh shit wait, I didn't mention that the girl was a princess, that's important later on."

"I'm interested. I love a good fairy tale." Jasmine smiled at me and shut her notebook, clasping her hands together. "Continue."

"The boy, however, was a mere peasant from a nearby village to the princess's castle. He looked up at the towers and wished he could one day be with the princess. The princess looked down on the town and wondered how life was for the townsfolk," I told. "But one day, the peasant boy took a journey to the castle and shouted to the window of the tallest tower. And the princess stuck her head out to see who was calling her name. The boy professed that he wished to take her hand in marriage, and the princess told him to go and buy her a sheep.

"And so the peasant boy worked for a month and bought a sheep. He brought the sheep to the castle and asked the princess for her hand in marriage again. She told him no, and that she wanted an entire *flock* of sheep. So the peasant boy went back to town and worked for a year and brought her a flock of sheep. She still refused his proposal. He asked what she would like from him. She told him she would like a beautiful and extravagant necklace with a gem that sparkles in the moonlight.

"And so the boy works and he goes searching for a gem that sparkles in the moonlight. It takes him another year to save enough money and to find the perfect gem. He heads back to the castle and as he places the necklace over the princess's head, he asks if she will marry him now. And she still says no, and says that he must bring her a bountiful and exotic treasure."

Jasmine's eyes were transfixed on me. I liked this feeling. I wished I could just tell a story forever and ever just to have her look at me with wonder and intrigue. Where was I going with this story? What was the message? The theme? The ending?

I continued, "The peasant boy spends six months working and saving money for his travels and he goes out on an expedition. He spends five whole years away, and by this point, he is a man, strong and courageous and he returns to the village as a hero. He arrives at the castle gate and again asks the princess to marry him."

"And she says no?" Jasmine interjected.

"No," I told her. "The princess says yes, but only after he brings her a castle's worth of servants. And so the peasant man gathers a battalion of men from the village and takes them on a conquest of a foreign village, bringing back peasants in chains. And now the peasant man is a hero, a commander of the armed forces in the kingdom. He is wise beyond his years and he gifts the servants to the princess. And the princess tells the man that she does not love him and so they do not get married.

"The man is hurt and asks how could it be that she still after all this time doesn't want to marry him. He had done everything she had wished for, brought her everything she had wanted from him, given so much of his life and youth to the pursuit of being with her." I paused and looked at Jasmine. "And that's the end."

"Why did he just assume the princess would fall in love with him? They barely knew each other?" Jasmine asked.

"It was a different time. That's just what they did back then."

"So why didn't she marry him, then?"

I shrugged. "She didn't love him. One is loved because one is loved. Material items can't purchase love, and if it can, then that wouldn't be *love*. That's the moral of the story."

"That's a good moral."

"Yeah, I mean, I guess so. I just thought of the story as I made it up, so the moral sort of had to come out of nowhere."

Jasmine blew a raspberry. "I have a story to tell you as well, actually. And it also involves a beautiful princess."

"Well," I said, "lay it on me." I took in the momentary pause as she stopped to think of the proper way to start her tale. The wind flowed around us and flicked the strands of her hair out of her face.

"Okay."

"Okay."

"So, it was a bright and sunny day in the kingdom by the lake, and the princess in her castle was feeling rather glum. She went down yonder to the nearby river to find the castle's jester, who often rested on the shore. She asked the jester for a story to pass some time. And the jester happily obliged. And so the story went like this:

"It was a bright and sunny day in the kingdom by the lake, and the princess in her castle was feeling rather glum. She went down yonder to the nearby river to find the castle's jester, who often rested on the shore. She asked the jester for a story to pass some time. And the jester happily obliged. And so the story went like this:

"It was a bright and sunny day in the kingdom by the lake, and the princess in her castle was feeling rather glum. She went down yonder to the nearby river to find the castle's jester, who often rested on the shore. She asked the jester for a story to pass some time. And the jester happily obliged. And so the story went like this—"

"Is that the whole story?" I asked. "Does it just repeat?"

Jasmine nodded. "It's a never-ending story. That's the point. It's a cute joke."

"It is. I'll have to remember that one."

"Put your own twist on it though," she told me. "That version is *mine*. I own the copyright to it because I came up with it. But you can make your own." She smiled. "Or just say you're retelling a beautiful and wonderfully moving story told you by the one and only Jasmine Hudson."

I smiled at her. And she smiled back. And the wind pushed her hair around and I felt it pushing my hair softly, a gentle brushing. The smell of grass and summer filled the air and she opened her notebook and began writing again. And so I followed her lead and opened my notebook.

EIGHT

The evening was dawning on the camp. I guess setting? Settling? It was evening. The sun was sinking below the treeline
and I was happily in my dorm room after dinner. I was scrolling Facebook, Twitter, all the dank and/or spicy memes the
internet has to offer. I probably spent more time aimlessly
scrolling websites than I did writing. I should write all the
time, but procrastination is always a writer's best friend and
mortal enemy.

Well, that *and* a healthy bout of writer's block.

And that's what befell me that fateful evening. And so I
dulled the ache with mindless scrolling of websites. Everybody does it. That and because I just wanted to reflect on the
wonderful afternoon I spent with Jasmine, just the two of us
in the field, telling stories and writing in our notebooks. I
would have loved it if the afternoon never ended, if the two of
us could have just stayed there like that forever.

Maybe in some other life, I could be the prince to her

princess and she could ask me to tell her stories by the river shore in the kingdom by the lake. I would have liked that, or maybe we can at least play pretend and I can make her a flower crown and we can sit with the waves of this camp's lake lapping at the soles of our feet. In another life, maybe Jasmine and I would be the prince and princess in *this* kingdom by the lake.

"Wake up, Dee," Taron's voice boomed into my room.

I turned around so fast my earphones got caught on my body and ripped out of my ears. I let out a small yelp as I winced. "What's up?" I asked, noticing that Seth was just behind him in the doorway.

"We're going on an adventure," Taron explained, "and we'd like you to come with us, bud. 'Cause both Seth and I agree that you can't stayed holed up in this room all summer long. And so we're going to make sure you don't."

"I was outside today," I told them. "Where were you two? Holed up in your rooms?"

"He was, maybe," Seth chimed. "Come on. We have a place we wanna show you."

"A place? Is it cool?"

"I only know cool places." Seth did some finger guns. "Okay." He nodded for me to get up. "Let's get moving, dude."

"Yeah, sure." I shut my laptop and grabbed a long-sleeved T-shirt. I swapped shirts and was ready to brave the vast outdoors once more. I noticed that Seth and Taron both had their backpacks on. "Should I bring anything?" I looked right at the backpacks so they would know why I was asking.

"Your workbook, a sweater, pencils and pens, I dunno. Just bring what you think you should," Seth replied.

"Make it snappy though," Taron added.

I pushed my notebook into my backpack and I stuffed a sweater in there with it. I put a water bottle and a protein bar I bought from the cafeteria (yeah, the cafeteria sells protein bars here, weird) into my bag. "Let's go."

47

The walk was short. Not much happened. None of us really talked because I doubt they wanted to have me ask where we were walking to for the entire duration of the walk. But they were taking me into the forest, a fair way into the forest, away from the prying eyes of the other campers and teachers, into a world populated by squirrels and foxes and tall oaks. Something about the forest really did feel isolated, like we had stepped into a whole other country. The camp was a distant memory to this place. Humans were even more distant. But yet there was a worn track in the ground of campers having come through here every summer for X amount of summers.

I liked the forest. Always have liked forests. Something about the lonely feeling it gave me. I felt safe and vulnerable at the same time. The thicker the trees, the better for the feeling. I loved looking into the vast distance and seeing nothing but trees. The light wasn't harsh, the air was cool, and the sounds were relaxing. I loved it. My friend's backyard borders a small woods and we spent a lot of time in there, building forts and pretending we were soldiers in Guadalcanal (which was a battle in the Pacific Theatre of the Second World War, and we learned about it through this WWII video game we used to play).

"Whatcha thinking about?" a voice asked.

I turned and replied, "The forest."

Jasmine smiled. "You seem very lost in thought about it."

"Where did you come from?"

"Brighton, Ontario, from my mother's womb."

"No, I mean, why are you in the forest? Where did you come from?"

She grinned. "I was at the place Seth and Taron are taking you too."

"Why are they all the way up there?" I asked, noticing that they were a good hundred or so feet ahead of where

Jasmine and I were standing.

"You zoned the fuck out. You just stopped and started looking at the treetops and I was passing by and they told me to tell you to get a move on," she explained, the subtly breeze playing with her hair. "Not like they care, standing around and talking is their favourite pastime."

"It's quickly becoming mine," I told her, forgetting to add the part that mentioned that it was my favourite if it were her I was talking to.

"Well, you should be going." She smiled and rested a hand on my shoulder. "And stop zoning out while you're walking. It's not safe in the forest. You might get attacked by a wild fox out here."

"If I die in a fury of red fur and tricksy den scrapers, so be it."

She started laughing, a cute little laugh at first, but her laughs kept building up until she was reaching a hand across her stomach and snorting for air. She closed her eyes when she smiled. And her nose crinkled and the starburst between her eyes made me feel like my heart was about to burst the same way. "Tricksy den scrapers?"

I nodded. "They're tricksy and they scrape dens."

"I like you, Dee." She smiled again, still a little out of breath from her laughing fit. "I should get going."

"You can come hang with us, if you want to?"

She shook her head. "Nah. They're not my friends, they're yours. And besides, I was just there, I'm secret placed out for the day." She smiled once more. "But I'll see you later."

I turned and watched her walk away. I wondered what she thought of me. If she thought I was cute. If she noticed the way I smiled like I noticed the way she did. If she liked my eyes. If she marvelled in the way my hips swayed when *I* walked away from her. If she liked the way the wind moved *my* hair. If she found warmth in the way *I* pulled petals off of flowers and weeds.

I caught myself ogling and had to stop myself. As nice as Jasmine's frame from behind was, I had to catch up to Seth and Taron before I was left behind in my daydreams.

"Let's gooooo," Seth's voice echoed through the forest as I started walking towards them. "We want to show you this cool place we go to, not the forest. 90% of this province is forest, for Christ's sake."

"Yeah, yeah," I muttered as I caught up to them. They took a sudden and abrupt left turn towards where the lake would be. We walked a little further and I saw the shoreline of the lake come into view. The trees broke away from our sides and there sat a shaded beach and a small wooden shack that had more than likely seen better days.

"I now present to you, the Nutshack," Taron said, opening his arms in gesture towards the ruddy shack.

"It's not called the Nutshack, and I hate that dumb meme," Seth groaned. "It's called the Writer's Shed. Because apparently even with all these creative writers around, the least original name won out."

"And I've been trying to rename it ever since I knew about this place," Taron added.

"So why doesn't *everyone* just come down to this place all the time?" I asked, getting the obvious out of the way.

Seth sighed, and Taron replied, "Because most people don't like coming out here because it's too far into the woods, there's a fuck ton of mosquitos in the evening—bring bug spray,—and because they simply don't like it. It's more a poet's shed. Poets, like Jasmine, and loners, like Seth and I, enjoy this place because it's quiet and whatever."

"And because honestly, camp gets boring," Seth noted.

"Yeah, what's life without a few bear attacks?" I joked.

"Oh, you read the camp brochure I see?" Seth laughed. "There's no bears near here. The camp makes sure of that. They get shooed off into the rest of the forest. The fish are big though. Those might attack you." Taron wiggled a finger around in front of his crotch as Seth continued. "Might mistake a part of your anatomy for a tasty snack. S'all I'm saying."

"So… why aren't you guys friends with Jasmine?" I asked.

"You mean friends anymore," Taron added.

"Yes, I mean that."

"Well, it was a long time ago," Seth started.

"And the waters were rising fast," Taron added.

"Taron, shut up." Seth pushed him and took a seat on a fallen down tree, so a log I guess. Seth sat down on a log after pushing Taron out of the way. "I dated her friend. That's the story. We were all friends, the four of us, and then her friend and I broke up and her friend moved away and Jasmine blamed me for breaking her heart so bad she had to move to Nova Scotia. And then things were just awkward for Jasmine and me. This was last summer though, so we've had time to adjust and we talked about it. There's no blood between us, but we're not *friends* either."

"And I don't really care either way. I'm friends with her still," Taron stated. "I message her weekly."

"You do?" Seth asked.

Taron nodded. "I don't hang out with her because you were my friend first, but we were friends, so I just make sure she's okay and stuff."

"You're a good dude," I noted.

Taron shrugged. "Decency shouldn't need to be complimented, but thank you."

"You're welcome."

"Anyway, let's go explore the Nutshack." Taron walked over to the old wooden door and pulled it literally off its hinges and moved it to the side. "It's easier than opening it. Trust me."

The inside of the Poet's Shed smelt like dust and grass. The interior looked like maybe it had been nice once, but not recently. There was a bed, some plastic chairs, a few desks (all of which were free of dust), and another door leading to a room that looked like a makeshift outhouse. I guess because people didn't wanna go into the woods to relive themselves. All those things aside, I could see the charm in this place. It was a little forest grotto, hidden away from the world, forgotten by those who built it, and left to future writers to decide its fate. And for the past X number of summers, the campers have kept the Poet's Shed alive.

The smells of past sex, drugs, and vomit were still hanging in the air. Some part of me wished I could know every story that unfolded here. Another part of me wished I could write my own story of sex, drugs, and vomit into the dusty floorboards. Perhaps someday, maybe.

Seth pulled a box out of his bag and set it on the floor. The game was Scrabble. Because we're writers. So of course it was Scrabble. Not that it matters. I'm undefeated in Scrabble.

NINE

This was no ordinary Tuesday, except that it was a very ordinary Tuesday. Our third Tuesday of the summer. I woke up bright and early and drank coffee that I made in the common area with a single-cup brewing machine. I finished reading the last little bit of *The Alchemist* by Paulo Coelho. One of my favourite books, so I find myself reading it a lot.

I love what the book says about finding our Personal Legends. We're all out there, looking for our treasures in our own way. I wonder if I've found mine, or if I ever will. If it's my books or if it could be Jasmine or Taron or Seth or if I'm too young to even understand what this world has in store for me. Sometimes, I have to remind myself, like really remind myself, that I'm only sixteen and that there's so much in life left to do. Nothing in my life is final right now. Life is wide open, with my Personal Legend waiting for me somewhere out there. Or I can at least I had a Personal Legend out there waiting for me somewhere.

Anyway, I made my way to class and sat next to Seth. He made it a point to be there first, before anyone else, so he could get the best seat. And then I, as his new friend, got the second-best seat—the one next to him. The morning wasn't the cool part of the day however.

The afternoon was. It's the part of the day when we don't have class with people of our own writing group. That means: I had class with Jasmine in the afternoons, though we never really spoke because she sat with her friend, the one with the light brown hair that I saw with her at the orientation assembly.

I mean, there's nothing inherently special about having class with someone on this day when I've had class with her since the start of camp, or even having class with her at all wasn't that special. There's only 41 kids at this camp, so the odds were in my favour to have class with her since classes here were only in groups of 10.

I don't know if I went over it, but there's 10 freshmen, 10 sophomores, 11 juniors (my group), and 10 seniors. There was supposed to be 11 seniors, but someone dropped out the week before camp started. And amongst each of us, they try for 4 writers, 3 poets, 2 comics, and 1 whatever else, playwright or screenwriter or what have you. The comics and whatever elses were grouped together for morning classes, poets were grouped together, and so were the writers. Smaller classes meant more one-on-one time with the instructors to hone our craft. But enough *about* class, that's not what this class was about.

Jasmine was sitting in her usual spot in the row closest to the windows. The instructor was droning on about zines and how zines are actually an important form of literature and art because it represents the purest form of our expressions and about how people will find any means they can to get their zine from their mind to the paper.

I wasn't paying any attention. Neither was Jasmine, which was evident because she was happily conversing with her friend in the chair behind her. And the instructor did not like that one bit. She got angry at Jasmine.

"If you're going to talk in my class and disrupt other students, I do not want you in this glass." Her voice was shrill and sharp. "Now get out. You are excused until tomorrow when you're ready to be an observant learner."

I watched her walk out the door, her small round bum held in place by a tight pair of jeans. I figured that this was a good time for me to get kicked out of class as well. So I stood up tall and stared at the instructor. "She was talking. That's what we're here for. We're here to meet other writers and poets. We're here to collaborate, not learn about folded pieces of paper with fancy black-and-white photos on them."

"Out. Come back tomorrow with a proper attitude." The instructor narrowed her eyes at me, watching as I picked up my backpack and headed into the hallway. Jasmine was just opening the door to the outside, so I ran and caught up with her out there. The entire run to the outside, I was thinking of how this was a strike against me. A "strike" against me. They don't kick anybody out. Strikes just equate to teachers being less likely to like you.

She turned around upon hearing my feet slapping against the gravel. "What are you doing, Dalton?" She didn't sound unhappy with me being there, but she was genuinely and pleasantly surprised.

"I couldn't let you get kicked out of class by yourself."

"That's very Alaska of you," Jasmine said. Now that I thought about it, me getting thrown out of class is pretty much exactly like what Alaska did for Pudge in *Looking For Alaska*.

I smiled. "It's what I do."

"Well, come on. Let's go find a watering hole. I'm thirsty." She smiled and offered her hand to me. I took it and we walked. Her skin was soft and warm and even though the air was warm, her warmth was giving me those goosebumps usually saved for cold days and hot cocoa. And she smelled of vanilla and gardens, or maybe just vanilla. We were approaching a flowerbed and small pond.

"Do you drink from this pond?" I asked her.

She blew a raspberry. "Sometimes. Not today. I left my water bottle here at lunch, so I'm gonna drink from that."

"So what do you do here?"

"Talk and write and eat snacks and stuff. This is my hideaway." She motioned to a thicket of bushes and small trees that bordered one side of the pond. I followed her as we walked into the shrubbery. There was a cave of sorts inside the greens. It was amazing. It looked like someone had made an igloo out of a bush. And it was actually pretty spacious. "This is my garden." Jasmine motioned towards another opening where I could see a sunny patch of green plants. There were trees bordering it on each side, hiding it from the rest of the wide open field.

"Your hidden garden."

"A garden of eatin'," she joked, pulling a granola bar from her sweater pocket. A sweater with sleeves far too long for her small arms.

I looked around for a place to sit. There were a few twigs in here, but not much of anything to sit on. "What do you do in here?"

"I tend to my garden," Jasmine replied. "Wait here." She walked into the garden and disappeared from view for a few seconds and then reappeared with something round and green in her hands.

"Is that a lettuce?" I asked.

She shot me an offended look. Her eyes were wide and her mouth hung open. "How dare you assume his veggie-type. He is a cabbage."

"And it's a he?"

Jasmine nodded. "His name is Fred."

I cocked an eyebrow and softly chortled. "A cabbage named Fred. I never would have guessed I'd meet a cabbage with a name before."

"I give names to the things I think are cool and call them friends," she replied. She held the cabbage, Fred, out towards me. "Go on, say hi. He won't bite."

"If a cabbage could bite, I would not let it bite me," I told her. Though every pet I've ever had bit me, a cabbage should be a little different I would think, seeing as it doesn't have teeth. Anyway, I took the cabbage from Jasmine's arms and held it like a baby, because how else are you supposed to hold a cabbage? I was weary of its leafiness. It was warm, it was in the sun. "So, when did you plant these? Camp only started a few weeks ago."

"I snuck in before camp started, back in the spring. My parents were cool with it and my best friend's dad is the owner of the camp." Jasmine smiled, watching me standing in the shade of her hideaway whilst holding a freshly picked cabbage. An infant cabbage. I held it gingerly and I felt the eyes of Jasmine on me as I rocked it back and forth a little bit. It was just reflex, I guess. Like how when you hold a baby you kind of sway back and forth. I haven't held many babies in my life, but it feels like that's what you're *supposed* to do.

"That's pretty cool."

"Cool that I have a garden or cool that I snuck into camp in the spring?"

"Both." I handed Fred back to Jasmine. "So what was it like in the spring? Does it look any different?"

"Not really. Just wetter, I guess. Everything was all melted and it had rained a lot before I came here. I guess it felt more nature-y. No other people but me and my mom, so I guess that was cool, being alone out here like that." Jasmine started rocking Fred back and forth slowly as well. I don't know if it was to mock that I had done the same, or if it was a show of solidarity, or if she had just always done this with cabbages.

And I wondered how many cabbages she had given growth to. And how many she named and called a friend. Maybe there's a Susan, a Trevor, a Carrie, a Mark. All cabbages. Maybe this is the first time she's ever grown and named a cabbage.

As I watched her sway with Fred in her arms, I had never wanted to be a cabbage so badly. I wanted her to wrap her arms around me, squeezing me as tight as she could and letting me pick her up off her feet and spin us around in a bear hug.

And I suppose my mind took a daydream approach to this bush cave we were in and situation in front of me.

All light fell from around Jasmine and I, the world was blackened and only the two of us were lit up. And the dirt was hardwood floors. And there was a swelling of soft music, just loud and fast enough to invite us to dance. And I raised my hand and her delicate fingers graced mine with her touch and I pulled her closer. I rested a hand on her hip, imagining how my hand would fit her curves. Her hands on me. Our eyes locked, and our feet moving like we were the same machine. The music swelling and we would trot to the beat. One two three four, one two three four, one two three four, one two three—

"Dalton!" Jasmine shouted.

My eyes spun around their sockets and landed on Jasmine. She was kneeling on the ground with Fred in front of her and a Sharpie in between her fingers.

"I want you to give Fred a face." She held the marker out towards me. "But you have to make it pretty. Fred doesn't wanna be ugly and *we* don't want to make him ugly either."

I took the marker from her and smiled. I was past the fact we had a cabbage named Fred, or even that we had a friend that was a cabbage. I was just lucky enough to be let in on Jasmine's secret garden hideaway, so you better believe I drew Fred the prettiest face you had ever hoped to see on a cabbage.

TEN

God, she was beautiful. Her legs crossed in the grass, the blades barely touching her skin. Her pink-painted toes wiggled in the green and she smiled at herself as she wrote in her notebook. Her skin glowed even in the shade. She radiated the very essence of what I found beauty to be, and I didn't know what I found beauty to be until I looked at her. Her hair was down in front of her face, a bundle of it pushed behind her ear, but it didn't help much to keep it in place.

And fuck... she just looked so at peace, so carelessly wonderful in this moment. I couldn't even begin to explain it. I got lost in her, whether it was her eyes or her skin or her legs or the way she closed her eyes when she smiled, I just got lost in it all, in her.

If I could, I would tell you just how special she was. But words don't do it justice. And sure, I've know her for two and a half weeks, but in those two and a half weeks, she's proved to be something amazing. I'm allowed to appreciate her outer appearance, it was what drew me in, and now the person she is draws me in further. Curiosity killed the cat, *but satisfaction brought it back.*

"Are you staring at me?" Jasmine's head perked up and she looked at me.

My mouth fumbled for words and my cheeks went red (I assumed since they suddenly felt like they were on fire). I sat there, looking at her, with my notebook open to a blank page and I had no words. Until I said, "Maybe."

"Yes or no?" Jasmine's eyes narrowed at me and she closed her notebook. "I won't be mad if you were. Be honest."

I sighed. *Fuck.* "Okay, yes. I was. I just zoned—"

"You're cute." She smiled. "I find it a little endearing when boys stare at me. And I find it cute when they blush for getting caught." She hopped upright before I could say another word. She left Fred on the ground and she started for the exit to our bush cave. "Come. We're gonna go to the dock. Fred wants a nap and I wanna dip my toes in the lake."

The lake was a small one in comparison to other lakes. You could swim across it without being too tired, I suppose. It was big enough that there was a healthy fish population though, and deep enough that there was a floating dock several dozen feet out from the shore for people to dive off of. Jasmine and I sat on the dock that was attached to the shore though. A rickety wooden contraption that floated and bobbed with the water. I felt like it might break away from shore and float into the lake, but Jasmine was sitting next to me, so I guess floating out there wouldn't be so bad with her by my side. I knew how to swim, so getting to shore wasn't a big deal.

"Whatcha writing?" Jasmine asked, her legs swinging back and forth, her toes barely touching the water, but touching enough to cause little ripples

"I dunno. Book ideas I guess." I sighed. "They're not very good."

"Sure they are. All ideas are good."

"Unless they're not."

"But I'm sure they are. All ideas are good."

"Unless they're not." And before we began an endless cycle, I said, "And mine aren't good. We're not all as smart and creative as you."

"I'm gonna disagree to agree."

"That's not the saying."

Jasmine glared at me. "Do you think fish want to walk on land?"

I watched as she wiggled her toes in front of a fish. The fish didn't go for it, no bite. "I think fish don't think anything," I told her. "Fish just live, they just *exist*."

"I wanna be a fish." Jasmine sighed and looked at the shiny little fish. I don't know the species. Maybe trout? It wasn't cute. It wasn't like the guppies you keep in your home fish tanks.

"But why?"

She shrugged, letting her hair fall down her back. "I guess I, like fish, want to just exist and float through space and time. And breathing water would be cool. You'd never be thirsty if you literally breathed water."

"You're making being a fish sound cooler than it is."

"Being a fish *is* cool, Dee. I don't have to make something cool sound cool, it already is cool." She kept taunting the fish with her toes. The fish probably knew enough to know that humans aren't food. "I'd wanna be a betta fish or something though. They're tough."

"Fish eat their own poop," I noted.

"I refuse to be swayed. I want to be a fish."

"Do you like swimming?"

"Not particularly."

"But you wanna be a fish?"

She nodded. "Well, I need something to complain about

still, and if I was a fish, I could complain that I had to swim all the time."

"You confuse me." I closed my notebook and looked over at her. "Did you get a lot of writing done?"

"Always."

"That's good."

"I find you easy to talk to."

"Thanks," I told her, "I think." Was that a compliment? Humans are social creatures. We invented language for that reason. Shouldn't we all be easy to talk to unless we speak different languages? I guess she just means she feels comfortable talking to me. It's still a weird concept. It's easy to talk. We do it all the time, I guess was my point.

"I guess I just like being around you." She smiled softly. "I don't have anyone that I can just sit around and write with. I mean, I have Shelby, but like, it's different. You let me write. I let you write. We write together and it's not weird. I love it, actually."

"Oh, well, for the record, I love it too," I told her. And I meant that just as much as she did. It was so nice to have someone to write with.

"I'm gonna get going. Class probably got out not too long ago. I wanna go see Shelby." Jasmine sighed a little and kept taunting the fish. It's like she was trying to play with the fish, but the fish didn't wanna play. "Anyway, I'll see you around, Dee." She leaned down and pulled my face upwards to hers and she kissed me on my forehead.

Her lips were soft on my skin. Warm too. It sent shivers down my spine, electricity through my bones. I felt more at peace with her lips on my forehead than I have ever felt in my entire life beforehand. I closed my eyes and let the warmth of her lips take me over. I wished she would take my shut eyes as a sign to kiss my lips, but the forehead kiss was plenty good enough. It relaxed my entire body, my entire soul. She stopped and stood up straight. She smiled softly and then walked off down the dock.

And that was that. The first time Jasmine's lips ever touched any part of my body. And for perhaps the first time in my life, I didn't want to be someone else. I didn't want to be somewhere else. I wanted to be right here, right now, and I sure as hell wanted to be me.

I guess in the story, the essence of how much of a loner I was before this camp was lost. Remember, I sat in the back of class and listened to the other people live their lives. I never got to kiss the cheerleaders or play on the football team or go to the parties. That just wasn't my life. I was always the outsider looking in, wondering what it was like. I was always the observer. But at this camp, I'm part of something. I'm a piece of the puzzle we're all building.

In two weeks, I had a crush and two quasi-friends. That's pretty impressive from a kid just a few weeks removed from being the most unassuming and least interesting kid in high school. Seriously, even the band geeks have more going for them in terms of coolness. And all they do is practise their instruments in the band room.

"There you are," Taron's voice shouted to me.

I craned my neck back. "I am here." Seth was walking with him. They looked both pleased and displeased with me at the same time. I don't know how to describe it other than that.

"I hear you ran out of class after Jasmine," Seth stated. "May I ask why?"

I shrugged. "Because I had to follow her."

"He's smitten, eh. Let him be." Taron sat down next to me. "Lot of fish here today."

"Don't change the subject," Seth barked as he sat down on the opposite side of me. "I'm warning you about Jasmine. She seems cool, but she's selfish and far too absorbed in her dumb poetry than in you or anybody else."

"That's not true," I stated. "She likes spending time with me."

"She just hates being alone," Seth muttered. "I'm just

saying that you should be careful. I know she's enticing with her olive skin and luscious hair and all that other lame shit, but trust me, girl's trouble for a romantic like you."

"Who said I was a romantic?"

"You walked out of class after her. You got *kicked out* of class for her," Seth stated. "I suppose that would be evidence number one."

"I'm happy for you, buddy," Taron said, resting a hand on my back.

"I am too. Like, if you like her, by all means." Seth sighed. "Just warning a dude so he doesn't go in blind and get chainsawed by his first summer love."

"I'll be okay," I told them.

"So what'd you two do with all that free time?" Taron asked, genuinely interested in hearing about my day, which was nice for a change to have someone actually *want* to listen to me.

I shrugged. "Pretty quiet and relaxing. I drew a face on a cabbage and we wrote together in our notebooks and she told me she wished she could be a fish."

"Weird," Taron said. "Fish are weird." He was looking right down into the lake now, right at a small group of fish that were swimming in the shade of the dock. "So you like Jasmine, huh?"

I shrugged. "She's cool."

"But how do you really feel?"

"When she laughs, I feel like every problem in the world fades away. When she laughs, my hearts feels warm and light and everything is okay and there's nothing else that matters. When she laughs, it melts me. When she smiles, the world goes dark and it's just her, it's just her and me. When she speaks, that's all I can hear, and it's music to my ears."

"You have a crush," Seth teased. "How cute."

And then they a sang. They sang an entire song at me. The *entire* song *Summer Nights* from *Grease*. Despite me begging them to stop, they duetted the entire thing at me. I don't know why or how they have the whole thing memorized or why they sang it so perfectly together or even how many times they had sung it together before. Maybe this was one of those rare moments in life where the unspoken bond of friendship created a beautiful moment. Or Seth and Taron just share a brain. That sounds about as realistic.

"Come on. I hear they're having ice cream in the caf today," Taron said.

And so we all went and got ice cream. Cookie dough for myself, mint chocolate chip for Taron, and vanilla for Seth. I think I saw Jasmine with a mint chocolate chip cone too.

ELEVEN

Seth and Jasmine used to be friends. Fact. And things are awkward because Seth and her friend broke up. Fact. But they're both mature human beings and should be able to be friends without it being awkward. Fact. And now they have a mutual friend in me. Fact.

With all these facts, it's hard to see how they still think it's not a good idea to be friends. Jasmine is surely over the heartbreak he caused her friend and Seth doesn't have a reason not to like Jasmine at all, to be honest. Not from the information I've gathered from them thus far.

"No," Seth replied.

"Come on. One hangout," I pleaded.

He sighed. He was steadfastly against hanging out with Jasmine because it would just be awkward for everyone. His whole avoidance of Jasmine really made it seem like maybe *Jasmine* was the girl he dated, not her friend. And that's why it was awkward for them, and that would have made sense. But instead, Seth is just being a baby.

"I think it might be a good idea for you two to hang out," Taron added from the couch. We were in the common area right now. Just hanging around. I was on the floor, leaning my back on the couch. Taron was lying on the couch. And Seth was in an armchair beside the couch and he was unenthused by our conversation.

Seth groaned. "Ask her. See what she thinks. If she wants to do this stupid thing, then fine, I guess I can try to be nice. But it's just weird. I've never really seen her as anyone other than my ex's best friend."

"See her as a person, bud. That's what she is," Taron chirped him. "I think she's down by the pond. She usually is. The four of us could have a game night."

"Or five if she wants to bring her friend," I said, not quite sure if I was referring to Shelby or to Fred, the cabbage I had drawn a face on just a few days ago.

"I'm cool with that," Taron replied. He looked over to Seth. "This hoser's cool with it too. 'Cause *I* said so, eh?"

Seth nodded. "Whatever, man."

"I wish I had that kind of control over him," I muttered.

Taron chortled. "Maybe someday."

The walk was short. It's not like this camp is very big. Jasmine was easy enough to find. She was with her friend, Shelby, but I couldn't see Fred. There were just two pretty girls sitting by the pond with their backpacks out. The sky was blue and bright, but yet a small cloud had hid the sun from sight.

"Hey, Dee," Jasmine said. She stood and whispered something to Shelby and then walked towards me. The distance closed surprisingly fast until we were close enough that I could see the amber flecks in her dark brown eyes. At this closeness, I could make out some individual strands of hair in her eyebrows even. They were bushy, maintained but still thick.

"Hi."

"Whatcha doing?" She was shifting her weight from foot to foot, not in an urgent or impatient way, just in a way that said she was happy and carefree today.

I fumbled for some words and then finally got them. "We're having a game night. Seth, Taron, and me, and we'd like it if you wanted to come and hang out with us."

"With Seth? Doesn't he, like, not like me?"

I shrugged. "He's gonna make an effort to try."

"Sure." She smiled, her beautiful lips stretching out and upwards. "I'd like that. It'll be nice hanging out with Taron at least." She paused. "And you too. I like *you*."

"So… meet us in the common area at eight tonight?"

She nodded. "At eight. Sounds good."

"Okay. See you then." I smiled. I turned away from her and began walking back.

"Wait, Dee."

I spun around and walked right back up to her. "What is it?"

"What game are we playing tonight?"

I hadn't even thought that far ahead. The board games here were all falling apart and honestly board games are a little bit lame. So I shrugged. "Truth or Dare, I guess. That's a good summer camp game."

"Okay. You better do some dares."

"I will."

"You better."

"I *will*." I sighed internally. "You better do some dares too. I don't wanna be the only one naked and drinking the spoiled milk in the cafeteria's fridge."

"I promise that if someone else dares you to drink the spoiled milk, I will drink some with you." She stuck her pinky finger out, so I wrapped mine around it. She smiled. "Solidarity, Dalton. I'm with you on this one."

"I really hope we don't have to drink spoiled milk." Our arms fell back to our sides.

She shrugged. "Well, at least if we both drink spoiled milk, we're guaranteed to have someone to kiss all summer. Nobody else would want to kiss spoiled milk mouths like us."

"Are you saying you wanna kiss me?" I asked.

Her eyes darted downwards. "No. Just speaking from experience. I knew a guy who didn't get any summer kisses because he was dared to drink some nasty drink concoction in his third week at camp. I just... I dunno, don't want you to suffer in silence."

"Thanks. I think."

"Okay. You may go. I'm gonna get back to Shelby. We're planning a book together about runaways." Jasmine smiled once more and turned around, and as she walked she said, "Eight o'clock tonight. I'll be there."

I smiled at the back of her and then I turned and headed back to be with Taron and Seth. Jasmine had made an offhanded joke about being stuck kissing me all summer. The only thing was that it was a *joke*. Of that, I was 100% certain. There's no way a girl like her would want to kiss me, regardless of if we both had milk mouth or not. For a split second my hopes were up, but they didn't stay there because the realist in me sees the world the right way. The way it's always been for me.

The day wore on and I was getting more and more excited about having us all together in the evening for a rousing game of Truth or Dare. Do you ever notice how time seems to slow down to a crawl when you're waiting for your plans? Like, you have a friend to visit at five, the entire first part of the day seems like it's dragging on forever.

But eventually it comes around. I walked out to the common area from the bathroom and saw Taron, Seth, and

Jasmine sitting on the floor. They were all gazing over at me like they had asked a question that only I had the answer to.

"Hi," Jasmine said first.

"Had to pee," I replied, coming over and sitting down.

Jasmine pulled out a box. "Here. One of my dorm-mates had this, so she let me borrow it." The box was black and shiny, and it read TRUTH-OR-DARE, THE CARD GAME.

"A card game version? Well, where's the fun in that?" Taron teased as he slid the box over to himself.

"You'd have shitty dares anyway," Seth taunted. "I like this idea better. Have you played this before, Jazz?"

"Nope." She gave an uneasy smile. It was tense between them because they were both so nervous of it being awkward that it was making it awkward. "So I figured what time better than now to give it a try."

"How are we gonna decide who goes first?" Taron asked. "I vote tallest to shortest."

"I vote lady's choice," Jasmine added.

I pulled the box over to me and opened it. "I guess we can go shortest to tallest."

"Are you doing that just to spite me?" Taron asked.

I shrugged. "Maybe." I pulled out the cards and arranged them into a few piles. Each card had both a truth and dare written on it.

"So Jazz first, then Taron, then Dee, then me," Seth said, pointing to each of us and trying to make sure we all understood the order of play.

"Okay." Jasmine pulled a card off the top of the pile closest to her. "Wait, I get to pick anybody I want for these right?"

We all nodded at her. Seth said, "Of course. What fun would it be if you couldn't choose your victims?"

"Pick me!" Taron beamed. He must really enjoy this game.

"Okay," Jasmine said, "truth or dare, Taron?"

"Mm, dare. Duh."

She drew a card. "Remove your socks and wear them on your hands for the rest of the game."

"Drawing cards is gonna be hard," Taron said as he swung his leg over to remove a sock.

Jasmine shrugged. "If you're nice, I will pick up the cards for you."

Taron smiled as he pulled his sock off. "Yeah, that'd be very nice of you." He repeated the process for his other sock and then had two very crude gloves. "Okay. So I guess it's my turn now. Jasmine, draw me a card please."

"Who do you pick as your victim?" she asked as she picked up the card and held it in a way that only Taron could see it.

"Seth."

"Oh, come on," Seth groaned.

"Truth or dare, bud?"

Seth blew a long raspberry. "I'll do a truth."

"Okay, then have you ever lied on a truth? If so, what was it and why did you lie?"

Seth thought for a second. "Okay, so it was like two years ago I guess. I was at a *party* with friends and we played. They asked if I had ever had sex. So I wanted to seem cool, right? So I lied and said I had, but I hadn't yet at that point in my life. I just wanted to seem like the cool, mature friend at the party, so I lied."

"I feel you," I told him. "I did that too. I lied once on a truth and said I got a blow job from a girl." I shrugged. "I just wanted to feel cool, like I wasn't missing out on life even though I was."

"Feels bad, man."

"Okay, Taron." I eyed him over. "Truth or dare?"

He locked my gaze. "Dare."

I looked at the card. "Make up a rap about me."

Taron groaned. "You're right. Let's have the ginger free-style rap." He let out a louder groan. "Okay give me a second." And so the three of waited. "Okay, give me a beat."

And so Seth gave him a half-assed beatboxing beat. "So you came to this camp, to learn how to write / now we're sitting here playing games tonight / you wear cool clothes and shoes / this game is better with booze / I'm sorry I can't do much rapping / but Dee, you're shit at unpacking." Taron shrugged. "That's all I got." And the four of us burst out in laughter.

"That was pretty good," Jasmine said, trying to hold back another round of laughter. We were all still laughing and smiling a little bit. "Seth, it's your turn. Draw a card and ask one of us something."

Seth drew a card and looked at it, and then looked at each of us. "Hmm." He looked back at the card. "Jasmine. Truth or dare?"

"Oooh." She pressed her index finger to her lips. She pressed softly on her lip. Very art blog worthy. I've never wanted to be a finger so badly. "Dare." She smirked at Seth, wondering just what the card would say.

"The card, and therefore I, dare you, Jasmine, to *kiss* the prettiest-slash-hottest person in the room."

"Anybody I find the most attractive?" she asked.

He nodded. "That is what the card dares."

"Hmm." She again put her finger to her lips to think. And then she looked at each of us. My entire soul was afire. My heartbeat was like a bird alight. I froze to the ground I sat on. And I watched and waited. Every piece of me silently begging for her to kiss me. But she didn't. She stood up and walked across the room to her backpack, and from the backpack she pulled *him* out: Fred. She walked back over and showed us all the cabbage that I had drawn a face on. She smiled. "His name is Fred, and he is my most favourite boy." She kissed Fred on the "lips" and then set him down next to her. "There. It's my turn now."

"A cabbage?" Seth teased.

Jasmine nodded. "I happen to like him very much. Anyway—" She paused and looked around at us. "—Dee. Pick your poison. Truth or dare?"

I sighed, blew a soft raspberry, and answered, "I'll do a truth."

"Okay, this one's pretty easy." She smiled at me. "Do you want kids, and if so, how many do you want?"

I shrugged. "I haven't really ever thought about it. I guess I do *want* kids at some point, but I dunno how many. Maybe just two."

"Just two? I want, like, five. I want a large family, and we'll all live out somewhere in the countryside with rolling hills of green grass as far as the eye can see." Jasmine smiled as she looked upwards, obviously in reverie. "A big country home with a big red door and bay windows all over the place and a wraparound porch and a balcony on the second floor. A place where I can write poetry in the shade of a big oak tree while my children play in the field."

"You answered his truth better than he did," Taron teased.

"I just know what I want out of life, that's all."

"That's true." Taron sighed. "Jasmine, may you pick up a card for me?"

She nodded. "Here you are." She handed him a card and he held it awkwardly in his socked hands.

"Jasmine."

She sighed. "Dare me."

"The card, and therefore I, dare you to remove your bra without removing your shirt." Taron set the card down. The male version of that dare was to go commando for the rest of the game. I'm glad he didn't choose me for that. There's nothing comfortable about bare-balling in jeans.

Jasmine scoffed. "You act like this dare is a challenge." She pulled her arms into the shirt she was wearing and within seconds she had pulled the bra through one of her sleeves. "Ta-da." She dropped the bra behind Fred. "Easy peazy."

Now, as a teenage boy infatuated with a teenage girl, I could not help myself from noticing the way her tight shirt showed off her un-bra'd boobs, and the way her nipples slightly poked up, not noticeably unless you noticed, and I noticed.

I drew a card from the stack. "Seth. Truth or dare."

"I'm gonna go with dare. Lay it on me," he replied.

"Kiss the player to your right." I looked over to Taron. "So that's Taron."

"Shit," Seth muttered.

Taron turned and puffed out his lips a little. "Come on, then. Plant one on me."

Seth groaned. "Okay." And within two seconds, Seth and leaned over, pecked Taron's lips, and then was back in his original spot. Two seconds.

"My turn!" Seth said, drawing a card. "Ooh, it's a make your own. Okay, Dee. Truth or dare?"

"Dare," I replied. "It's only fair."

Seth smirked. "This dare involves a little bit of truth."

I nodded. "That's fine."

"I dare you, Dee, to kiss the prettiest person in the room." He smiled at me and flicked his eyes toward Jasmine.

"Oh. Um. Yeah. Okay. I will." I looked at Taron, and he too flickered his gaze at Jasmine. Both of them very clearly wanted me to take this chance to just kiss the girl. I looked over at Jasmine and I swear to God she gave me a small nod, as if to tell me it was okay to kiss her.

And so I did. I leaned in. I pursed my lips and closed my eyes. My hand reached up and held her cheek, guiding us towards each other.

And I kissed her.

For a second or for an eternity.

To me, the two were one and the same.

TWELVE

There are a million and one ways to describe how it feels to be kissed by someone who you like very much. There are a million and two ways to describe the way her skin felt. There are a million and three ways to describe the way she smelt up close, the rawness of it all.

My body was numb.

My lips were tingling.

My bones were firecrackers.

And I was aloft in my own soul.

I had kissed her. And something inside me snapped and broke open, something inside me released wave after wave of untapped emotion. I've never felt so much from a simple kiss before. Never have I felt like the whole world melted away, not until I kissed Jasmine.

It wasn't so much the mechanics of the kiss. A kiss is a kiss is a kiss, there's not that much variation between them. You put your lips against another person's lips. The end. Sure, some people have dry lips or very wet lips or they're a sloppy kisser, but generally, going in, you know what to expect.

But it's the emotions that make the kiss so great.

It's knowing the other person wants to kiss you as much as you want to kiss them. It's feeling their enthusiasm as a re-action of your lips' movements against theirs. It's in the rush of blood you get to your groin. The phenomenal scent of "Yes, this is the right person to be kissing."

And so as I lay in my bed, looking up at the bland ceiling, I couldn't help but wonder if the urge to kiss me was as strong in her as the urge for me to kiss her was.

We didn't talk about it after. We finished playing our game. We went back to our own rooms. Nobody said a word about it. It could merely have been part of the game. But it wasn't. It couldn't have been. The way she smiled as I was turning to her and getting ready to lean in. There's no mis-taking that she gave me the sign; she wanted to be kissed by me. Any other girl would have just turned her head, blushed a little at being thought of as the prettiest person in the room, and then just let me kiss them lightly for a second.

But Jasmine kissed back. She didn't "accept" the kiss. No. She *kissed back*. We kissed long enough that Taron had to cough a little bit for us to snap back into the real world again.

We got lost in each other for the first time.

And I can't even describe it.

All I feel is fireworks in my bones and a tingling in my cheeks and rocket ships in my heart. And all this from one kiss in a silly game. It's like when she kissed me on the fore-head but magnified tenfold. I felt this feeling course through my bloodstream. I was hooked on her, because sometimes you just *know*. And I know. And I hope she knows too.

I fell asleep that night with a small smile on my face.

And her taste on my lips: honey and cabbage.

THIRTEEN

For some reason, I woke up exceptionally early that morning after truth or dare. It was barely five AM, but yet I lied wide awake in my bed. The morning's soft blue light cast a haze over my dorm room. I wasn't awake, but I was. I was in that weird in between stage.

But I can tell you for certain that I was conscious. I heard the sounds of bird chirping, so at least that was a good sign. It meant that somewhere, someone in the cafeteria was preparing a breakfast for us campers.

Pancakes. Warm, buttery pancakes. My mouth was watering. But how could I be so in love with pancakes when just barely seven hours ago I had kissed Jasmine on the *lips* with my *lips*. And here I am, thinking about pancakes.

I was also wondering why the hell I was up so early in the morning. We didn't even have class today. We had a guest speaker come in. An author. She/he was going to talk about how writing books has changed their life or something. But that wasn't until like noon. That's in seven hours. Me being up at five AM is a crime, or it should be if it hasn't been passed into law already.

I rolled over in my bed and stared at my empty room. It was so eerily quiet and unmoving. I think that's just because there's no "sunlight" yet. I trained my ears on the silence and found nothing but more of the same. Couldn't imagine anyone else in my dorms being up at this hour.

I got out of my bed and went to the bathroom. I saw Taron's door open. I figured that he was up then. I walked by his room and he was sitting at his desk on his laptop with a drawing tablet. I suppose he hasn't been to sleep if he's drawing. His curtains were drawn, so I doubt he knows it's morning either. I wish I could get that lost in being creative. I always find myself somewhere else when I write. It sucks, but I guess that's how I write.

Anyway, enough about that. I sat on my computer for the next few hours. Staring at a blank word document for most of that time. Scrolling dank memes the rest. I'm a shit creative person, to be honest. I need to be better at forcing myself to make things. Because even making shitty things would be better than making nothing at all.

The day was warm. The sky was bright and blue and full of white puffy clouds slowly moving across it in a screensaver-esque glossiness. The air was cool and refreshing. It was, by all accounts, a wonderful summer day. And I was, by all accounts, still not ready to go and sit in the sun for three hours listening to why writing novels is a life-changing hobby. It's not. I promise you.

My life is not all that different now than it was before I began writing. Like, sure, now I have something to do instead of watching television all day long, but that's about it. Even all my observations of other people could pay off in a career or something, so it's not like being quiet and eavesdropping was only beneficial to writing. The only life-changing thing about writing so far was this camp, but writing itself hadn't changed me.

Or maybe it had. I don't know. I don't care.

Walking outside into the camp square with my water bottle in hand, I noticed Jasmine sitting nearby. And this is when time seemed to stop for me, because locked each other's gazes. She was sitting at a picnic table in the shade. She looked at me and I watched her face light up, her lips curling into a small smile, and her eyes literally brightening. I'm sure all that happened to me too.

Jasmine stands up and waves me over. "Hi."

"Hi," I replied as I walked up to her. She was alone, and for some reason that was weird to me. She would have usually had her friend Shelby with her any other day, but not today apparently.

"Did you wanna sit and have a snack with me before this boring-ass author speech?" Jasmine sat back down and I sat down next to her. The wooden table was cool on my skin, untouched by the day's sunlight.

"What is it?"

"Sugar cookies. I made them myself."

"When?" I asked, taking one from the small plastic container full of them that she held out to me. I was asking her because I hadn't remembered her having cookies at any time before right now and she certainly didn't make them last night.

"This morning," she replied. "I got up super early and didn't have anything else to do, so I forced Shelby to let us into the kitchen so we could bake."

"And you made these."

She nodded and took a bite of one of the cookies. "Try one. Go on. Take a bite. I promise they're good."

I took a bite and chewed and then swallowed and then smiled. She was right. The cookies were very good. "I love them. What's in them?"

"Sugar, flour, vanilla extract, a hint of lemon, and love. Lots of love. Can't bake cookies without love." Jasmine smiled as she spoke. "That's something my grandma always told me. That I can't bake unless I put love into it, because if there's no love in it, then all the cookies will be burnt and gross and all the cakes will be too dry to be enjoyable."

"Your grandma is a wise lady."

"You've never met her."

"Well, not yet."

"She's a sweet little thing. She can't be taller than five feet, grey hair, but her skin is still soft and smooth for her age. I've been graced with good genes," Jasmine rambled. I could listen to her ramble on all day. "All the ladies in my family have wonderful skin late into their lives. Like, my mom is forty-five, but you'd never know it. She looks twenty-three. I hope I look forever young."

"Wow. So, is that why you look twelve?"

Jasmine snort-laughed, and my heart turned into a puddle of feelings. "Shut up, Dee. You're the one who kissed a twelve-year-old last night then."

"Pfft."

"So this one time, I tried to make sugar cookies with brown sugar and I followed the recipe, but they melted and just, like, kinda boiled. My cookie pan was a mess of flattened, bubbling cookie dough. I was distraught. It was like cookie brittle. Sad and pathetic. A waste of good brown sugar."

"You didn't make them with enough love," I teased.

She sighed. "Fuck. You're probably right." Her lips stretched into a small grin.

I took another cookie and we sat together in the silence. The wind blew around us and between us and carried our emptiness to somewhere else because even though nothing was being said, the air was full of energy from the both of us.

And look, between you and me, the cookies she made

weren't very good. They were far too lemony and far too buttery. They weren't fully cooked either. But you're wrong if you think I wasn't gonna eat six of those bad boys with a fucking smile stretched across my face. Me enjoying these terrible cookies made her happy, and all I wanted was for her to be happy.

"So do you wanna sit with me at this speech?" Jasmine asked.

I turned to her and got lost in her brown eyes for a solid minute before replying, "Yeah. I'd love that."

"Cool. I was hoping you'd say that. Shelby's sitting off with her dad for the speech and I don't wanna sit front row," Jasmine stated. "But I would happily sit in the back and eat cookies with you instead."

"That sounds wonderful."

"Well, let's go." She put the lid on the cookies before I could take my third of what would be six cookies. "I wanna get a good seat before all the good seats are taken."

We took our seats in the empty audience of chairs, and Jasmine set the cookies down on my lap as she got comfy in her chair.

She sighed. "I hate this. I hate camp. I'm sick of always having dirt in the wrinkles of my feet." She pulled her flats off and dusted the bottoms of her feet before putting her flats back on.

"Maybe if you wore socks and proper shoes," I teased.

"Yeah. But I like to feel, I dunno, open. Free."

"Dirt is a part of that."

"Dirt is a part of you." She grabbed the cookies back. "These are pretty good. I'm proud of myself." She took a bite of the cookie. "So, like, your book. What's the deal? Am I ever gonna get a live reading of it?"

"It's not done yet."

"So?"

"So it's not done."

"Read me the first paragraph?" Jasmine jutted her bottom lip out slightly. It was dusted with sugar cookie crumbs. How could I say no?

"No," I replied.

She furrowed her brows. "What do I have to do?"

"Make me more cookies." Of course I would read a paragraph of my book to her, but I had to make her work for it. And the cookies were kind of growing on me at this point.

"Okay, do you actually like them?" Jasmine looked down at the plastic container of them. They looked a lot more yellow in the sun. "I don't think I cooked them long enough. And I'm pretty sure I used too much butter."

"But you made them with love." I turned to her and smiled softly. "So of course I like them. Anything made with love is good."

"No, but they're bad." She sighed. People were beginning to fill up the seats around us, so naturally, our voices started to get a little more aimed at each other. "I just feel like I let myself down. I'm so bad at baking because I never follow the recipe. I always add my own tweaks."

"But that's good." I took a cookie. "Putting your own spin on stuff is cool. It makes something common a little more original."

"Fair."

"I like them." I did not like them.

"I like you."

"I like you too." I did like her too.

She nudged my leg. "How much do you think this speech is gonna suck?"

"I don't know. Maybe it'll be kinda good." I shrugged. "Maybe."

"But probably not. We should sneak out, go see Fred or something." She grinned at me. "Unless of course you actually wanna stay for the next two hours in the sun. Poor fair-skinned boy like you would burn nice and quick. So here's the plan: We sit for twenty minutes, I go to the bathroom and then you say you need to go to your room to get your sunscreen because you forgot and the sun is bright and hot."

"You've put a little bit of thought into this."

"We can sneak into the kitchen and bake more cookies," she offered. "*Good* ones this time."

I nodded. "Okay, deal."

The author came on stage exactly two cookies and seven minutes later. And from that point and for the following nineteen minutes, Jasmine interlaced her small nimble little fingers with mine and held my hand tightly. And then she went to the bathroom. And I got up two minutes later. Nobody asked where I was going, but I woulda told them I was getting sunscreen.

Jasmine and I met outside the cafeteria and she pulled a small key from her pocket. We went inside, locked the door behind us, and kept the lights off. It would have been the perfect time to make out and make love, but we were here to make cookies. We filled up two containers of them. One for her, one for me.

And that was that.

We made cookies.

Good ones this time.

FOURTEEN

Sometimes, I'm a cliché. Like the day I asked Jasmine to be my girlfriend. That was as cliché as they come, because look, as much as we try to avoid clichés and trash them, clichés are good. There's nothing, like, inherently bad about clichés. Okay. I've used that word too much.

Anyway, the day after the author speech was *the* day. I skipped out on my morning class because I wasn't feeling well (and it was probably because of how many cookies I ate yesterday). Or it was a bullshit excuse I gave to my teacher because I just didn't wanna get out of bed.

I wanted to just lay in my sheets and remember the feeling of Jasmine's fingers interlaced with mine. I wanted her to climb through my window and climb into bed with me. I wanted her to lay in my cavity of my arm and chest, right in the nook of me and she could rest her head upon my chest and listen to my heart beating. I wanted to be near her. I wanted to hold her. She made my heart feel like it was sitting next to a fireplace with a cup of tea.

And so of course I was gonna ask her out on a date, or just to be my girlfriend. Dating at sixteen is, like, holding hands in a park and getting a blow job in the closet of a shitty house party with kids drinking two beers at the same time so they could tell their friends the next day how they got wasted and crushed more than 20 shots of vodka. Pro tip: That many shots of vodka would basically kill you at sixteen. But you're right, you had 20 shots and then did a keg stand and finished the night off with six beers. You're so right.

ANYWAY!

Back to summer camp.

I had decided I was going to ask Jasmine out in the most cliché high school fashion: a good old-fashioned note. A simple yes or no.

And so I marched on into that afternoon class with all the confidence I could muster up (which wasn't much). Because, let's face it, though I'm pretty sure she likes me in *that* way, she also might not. And I don't want to have confused her being nice and quirky with being flirty and into me. So confessing my undying summer love to her and asking her out was a big risk, even if it was realistically a 98% sure thing.

I sat next to her desk in "class" and waited until everyone, including the teacher, had their heads buried in a book or writing project. I slid her the note. It was simple:

Hello. It's ya boy, Dee.

And I was wondering if you would like to go out with me?
Like, on a date or whatever.
Because I think you're kind of cute and stuff.
So what do ya say?

O Yes   O No

And yes, I dotted the I's with hearts. I'm lame, so what. Fight me about it. I watched from the corner of my eye as she unfolded the small slip of paper. My heart leapt into my throat. I've never felt so anxious. I've never sweat so much just sitting in a chair.

I saw and heard her click her pen so the tip would pop out so she could write. This was it. I heard a small and swift mark on the page. Then I heard some more writing. I was getting a little excited. Writing could mean a cute comment. And then my smile faded. Writing could also mean a brutal rejection. My fragile heart wasn't ready. She handed me the paper back and I unfolded it and set it out on my desk to read her new addition.

I thought you were never going to ask! I would love to. You can text me later and we can talk about it. Here's my number cuz you might need it — 343-XXX-XXXX

xoxo,
Jasmine

I wanted to get up and actually scream with glee. I mean, I sort of knew Jasmine would say yes, but still, you never know until you know. I contained myself for the rest of the class though. Jasmine snuck a few smiles my way, clearly just as excited that I had asked as I was that she had said yes.

After class, Jasmine and I went our own ways like normal. Nothing had to change between us, not yet anyway. I had made plans to meet Taron and Seth out by the baseball diamond anyway, so that's where I was heading. I saw the two of them tossing the dirty white baseball back and forth. A third glove was sitting up against the fence, just waiting for me to stick my hand in it.

I dropped my backpack down beside the fencing and picked up the glove. I walked out onto the pitch and waved to them. "Afternoon, friends."

"Afternoon, bud," Taron said, he tossed the ball my way and I snapped it out of the air with my gloved hand. "Nice catch, eh."

"Thanks." I threw the ball towards Seth. "So why do we play catch so often?"

"It's repetitive, Dee." Seth threw the ball towards Taron. "It's like a metaphor for life or some other dumb shit."

"It's either that or we just really like getting out in the sun and fresh air," Taron added. "That's why I like it."

"Or is it because you hope to finally get a tan so people stop putting sunglasses on when they're around you at night?" Seth teased.

Taron scoffed and tossed the ball to me. "I enjoy the feeling of being a literal shining star."

"Moonlight drowns out all but the brightest stars," I said as I dropped the ball (literally). "J. R. R. Tolkien wrote that." I threw the ball over to Seth. "And Taron is the star that the moonlight cannot drown out."

"Do you think at some point he'll reach a point of paleness so pale that he will literally just become translucent and/or bioluminescent?" Seth asked.

"Oh," Taron piped up, "you're using big-boy words now, huh?"

"Are you embarrassed because you can't spell words good and became a comic artist instead?"

"You take that back!"

Seth shook his head. "Not gonna happen."

"Then I guess I'll have to just kick your ass."

Seth laughed. "You couldn't on your best day kick my ass on my worst day."

"But I have Dee on my team. It's two against one," Taron stated.

"Whoa. Don't get me involved in your marital problems," I said. I raised my hand. "Sauce me the ball."

Seth threw the ball my way. "I still love him."

Taron smirked. "I know you do."

"Hey, so while we're on marital problems, let's talk about this." I pulled the note out from my pocket and held it up in the air.

"What in God's green Earth is that?" Seth trampled a patch of dandelions as he trudged over. He yanked the slip of paper from my hand, unfolded it, and read it. "No way!" He looked up to Taron. "Come here. Read this."

Taron walked over and took the note from his hand. "Oh, my. What does this mean?"

"It means our little boy is growing up," Seth teased, handing the note back to me.

"So what's going on? Have you texted her yet? Taron asked. "Have you planned a cool date night or anything?"

"Not yet, and no, I'm just gonna wing it," I replied. "Look, I could honestly just sit with her under the stars and she would love that. That's the kinda girl she is."

"Mm, no, girls like *doing* things. Like, being taken out on a date. Even if it is just sitting under the stars, *you* gotta really sell it," Seth told me. "Just trust me on that."

"I've had girlfriends before," I reminded him.

He sighed. "*Had.*"

"And you're single too, so shut up."

"Single by choice," he stated.

"Just not your own," Taron chirped.

Seth pushed him. "Anyway, just trust me. She's a cool girl until she's not."

I cocked an eyebrow. "What does that even mean?"

"She's careless until she cares," Taron said, adding a few mockeries after, like: "The sky is dark until it's bright. The water is cold until it's warm. The food is raw until it's cooked." For some reason, those were just hilarious to me. Maybe they just struck the right chords.

"Look anyway, I'm happy for you." Seth smiled at me and rested a hand on my shoulder. "Low-key though, if you think you have a chance to score, let me know. I always keep condoms on my persons. Well, in my dorm room in my backpack, but same diff, right?"

"You need to find some chill. Jazz is conservative," Taron stated.

"You've clearly never met her. She's as liberal as they come."

"I mean about love and sex and drugs."

Seth shrugged. "She's down-home from a small town. Is that a fair enough compromise for you?"

"Guys. I'm down-home. I have morals. *I* don't wanna sleep with her yet," I cut in. "That's a *me* thing. My choice."

"Good choice," Taron said.

"Mm, no. I disagree. Sex is fun," Seth noted.

"Sex *is* fun," I agreed, "but I can wait until *she* is ready. And who knows, maybe the two of us just won't work out as a couple. And there's the whole distance thing after camp ends that we'll have to deal with."

"Ugh, let's not talk about the end of summer right now. We're not even a halfway through. Enjoy the good life."

"He is enjoying the good life. He has us and Jasmine and sugar cookies and all the free writing time in the world," Taron stated with a smile. He looked up and raised a hand to his face to shield his eyes from the bright sky. "Like, he's soaking up this beautiful sunshine with his two best buds. We're all living the life."

"That's what summer camp is for," Seth said. "Living."

"Poetic nonsense courtesy of two teen boys barely through puberty," I chirped at them.

Taron looked back at me and grinned widely. "I think we're wearing off on him."

I shrugged. "Maybe. Now go back to your bases. I wasn't done throwing this ball around."

FIFTEEN

So there I was. Alone in my dorm room with fifteen minutes to spend inside my head. Alone in my room with the empty ringing in my ears to fill the sounds of the nothingness all around me. I'm pretty sure the clock stopped working and time had slowed to a crawl. My heart was thumping in its cage of bones and I was trying to keep my cold hands from being clammy.

I was even *pacing* in my room. I'm sure that given enough time I would have just dug a hole into the carpeting. I was already dressed up. A button-up shirt, a pair of nice jeans, clean shoes, and I was even wearing an undershirt. That's about as fancy as a sixteen-year-old gets.

I wondered what Jasmine would be wearing. Would she dress up at all? Or would she just show up in her comfy sweater and jeans? Would she be wearing her worn-in high tops and have her hair in a messy bun? A boy can do a lot of wondering in just fifteen minutes.

I wondered how much of a date this would be classified as. I mean, we're young and it's not like I'd be taking her out to a fancy dinner or anything. But a date is different to every person. Some people think just hanging out in their basement eating pizza is a date. Dating is subjective, I suppose.

There was a rapping at my door (like, a knocking). Taron walked in. "Oh, look at you. All spiffy and fancy, eh?"

"Okay, be honest. Do I look good?"

"She's seen you try to eat the cafeteria chili using a knife, bud" Taron noted. "If she agreed to go on a date with you, she's clearly not after your looks."

"She's after his mondo dong," Seth chimed in from somewhere in the hallway behind Taron.

Taron sighed. "Yeah, anyway, I wanted to see you off."

"That's nice of you." I said, straightening out my shirt.

"Where are you meeting her?

"By the pond where we met Fred," I told him. "You remember Fred, the cabbage she carries around."

"It's definitely a new cabbage every few days though, right?"

I nodded. "She has a cabbage patch, so she makes a new Fred every few days once the old Fred starts to get limp and gross-looking."

"Well," Taron said, "I'm glad. Mouldy cabbage is just gross. Anyway, do you have any questions?"

"Not really," I replied. "Like, I don't go on many *dates*, but like, when do you think is the right time to kiss her?"

"End of the night," Seth butted in. "Right as you're dropping her off and saying your goodbyes. As soon as you think about turning around, kiss her and then leave."

"Wow, you're giving him real advice?" Taron teased.

Seth scoffed. "Dee's my friend too. I want him to be happy and if Jazz makes him happy, then so be it."

"She does," I muttered. "So much."

"Give me a six-word reply to how much you love her."

"She's the colours in my garden."

"That's a good one," Taron added. He pulled a small bottle from his pocket. "This will make you smell nice."

I sniffed myself, my chest and armpits, and said, "But I already *do* smell nice."

"Not nice enough."

"He smells fine," Seth said, defending my honour.

"You can't smell him," Taron stated. "He smells like a boys' locker room."

"I do not!" I protested. Though I guess I did go heavy on the dollar-store body spray. It's not my fault I'm poor and need to mask the smells of puberty.

"Change your shirt." Taron reach backwards and grabbed something from Seth. "Here." He handed me a cleaner shirt. And this one was ironed!

"You don't have to help me this much," I said as I unbuttoned my shirt. I tossed it to the side and took the new shirt from Taron. I buttoned it up and then he spritzed me with the new (and better-smelling) cologne. "Thanks."

"No problem." He smiled. "You clean up pretty alright."

"Okay, well, I have to go and meet her now," I told them. "Thanks for the help. I assume you'll be waiting here for me when I get back so I can tell you all about it?"

"We're like the parents you always wanted but never had," Seth chimed in. I heard him shuffle a little in the hall and then he popped up directly behind Taron.

"Get out of here." Taron moved out of the way of the door. "Go impress the hell out of that girl."

The hot summer air had been replaced with the moist coolness of the evening. I could hear bugs making chirps and other assorted sounds. Fireflies (lightning bugs, depending where you live) began flying around at this point too. Little dots of light in the dark blue of the night. I waited under the bright light of the cafeteria entrance doors for Jasmine. This was the agreed upon meeting spot.

I waited in the light, swatting the occasional mosquito off of my exposed neck and wrists. After a few minutes, Jasmine's silhouette approached me and she came up into the light. She was in a tight black dress—almost a sundress, really—and had put dark red lipstick on. Her hair was in a tight braid down her back. She hadn't went *all out*, but this was basically all out.

"Hi," she said, her voice sweet and soft.

"Hi." I tried to keep my voice just as soft, but that wasn't possible. My voice just *sounds* rough. Always. Can't avoid it.

"You look handsome." Jasmine smiled and she stepped right up close to me. Looking down my nose, seeing her fill my frame of view, was all I could ask for. The gnats and mosquitos buzzed around us, but I didn't care.

"You look better than words can describe."

She grinned softly. "I can see that in your eyes."

"Can you?"

She nodded. "I brought you something."

"What is it?" I asked.

She pulled a small yellow flower form her purse. It was a dandelion. "Come here." She pulled my head down a little and gingerly stuck the dandelion's stem behind my ear.

"Oh, thank you, Jazz." I pushed the dandelion more firmly behind my ear so it wouldn't just fall out the second I turn my head.

"So where shall we go?"

"I have a place." I raised my arm and she put hers through the hoop mine formed.

"It's a nice night," Jasmine said, looking up through the trees up to the endless night sky. There wasn't a single cloud that night. Just an empty, diamond-dusted sky.

I nodded. "Any night is a nice night with you."

"Are you just gonna say corny stuff all night?" She looked over and smiled at me. I could barely see the smile because we were in the dark now, but I knew it was beautiful.

I nodded. "Probably. I like corny stuff."

"Good," she said, "I'd be sad if you didn't say lame stuff all night. I'd like to think you like me enough to be a corny li'l dork for me."

"Well, just call me Dorky McGee," I said, immediately regretting that I ever decided to learn a language and open my mouth to speak ever in my life.

Jasmine chortled. "You're a*dork*able."

"I try my best."

"You succeed," she said, stumbling over a small rock in the dirt.

I caught her mid-stumble. "Whoa, already fallin' for me, huh?"

"That's a good recovery for the Dorky McGee thing." Jasmine rolled her ankle around. "Okay, I'm good. They should really do more to uproot these rocks. I'm sick of tripping all the time."

"Yeah, we're writers, not athletes."

"Speak for yourself." She stopped walked and stuck her leg out in front of me. "Look at these toned bad boys. Soccer legs, hockey legs, bike riding legs." She moved her hand down her leg. "And I even shaved them today."

"They're very nice legs," I mustered up. Oh, how my teenage mind just wanted her to wrap her bare legs around my waist. How it wished for her to let me wear her thighs as earmuffs. *They're very nice legs,* I thought, *was an understatement.*

"Sorry. Let's continue our walk," she stated. "So I'm from Brighton, I feel like maybe I told you that, but I'm telling you again." She pulled me a little closer to her so her arm wasn't as stretched out. "Where are you from again?"

"Belleville, born and raised."

"Mm, I was born in Vancouver, actually. Richmond."

"When did you move to Brighton?"

She shrugged. "Few years ago. It was a big change, having to give up all my friends like that. And then I found this place and I met Shelby and then things were less shitty."

"Look at all these gnats," I noted as we walked into a clearing. The air was more gnat than air, probably.

"There's so many." She raised her hand out and the gnats flew away from her. "And look at the fireflies!" She pointed to a few little dots of blinking lights in the air. She took off towards the fireflies and shouted, "I'm flying like the gnats." Her dress flowing behind her and I just watched as she ran into the darkness.

I followed her into the darkness of the night, into the fields surrounded by trees. I would follow her anywhere, even through the darkness. I would follow her into the forbidden forests of every magical universe. That's pretty lame, but it's the truth.

Jasmine had this aura about her. She was like a magnet and I was a humble piece of scrap metal. I was just drawn into her without knowing why, and I went to her without asking why. Everything between us felt out of my hands. It felt like time was moving in leaps and bound while I was sitting in a car that I wasn't driving. I was just in the back seat, relaxing and enjoy the views as they rolled by. And I had to say, with Jasmine, every view was nice, so I didn't mind it.

And out here, lost in the glow of the fireflies, their swirling crescendo of flickering lights in the darkness, with Jasmine trying to catch one in her hands, life felt alright. It felt like I was in the right place at the right time for the first time in long time.

SIXTEEN

She was beautiful. I was watching her from my seat atop a low branch in a tree as she danced in the pale moonlight, though the devil was nowhere to be seen anywhere near us. No, because any place with her was as close to heaven as I would ever get.

And I know you're thinking it. About this story. There hasn't been a lot of drama, but there never is with these kinds of summer romances, these gooey sappy stories about falling in love. The falling in love is the story, I guess. But the thing with these stupid summer romances is that they're *summer* romances. Everything is perfect. Everything is hued in golden light. Everything is warm. Everything is butterflies. Not everything would stay that way for Jasmine and I. Not every story has to have a happy ending.

Anyway, we're back in.

Our first date was going pretty much how I thought it would. Jasmine was being, well, Jasmine, and I was being, well, me. I couldn't see her very well in the darkness, but there was enough light to be able to see her shadowy form dancing and pirouetting. I silently thanked her over and over again for not trying to drag me into the dance with her. I would have, but I don't like dancing. I'm one of those *too cool to dance* kinda guys.

"Come here," Jasmine demands.

"Am I in trouble?"

"Perhaps."

I stepped forward. "What?"

She wrapped her arms around me and smiled. "At least do me the favour of one slow dance?"

I smiled and nodded. "Slow dancing I can do."

"Do you ever wonder what happens to the people here when camp ends?" she asked as my hands found a place to rest on her hips.

"No, I haven't." And I guess that was true. Outside of her, I hadn't given a second thought about anybody at camp to begin with. Seth and Taron, sure, but not really anyone else. And I sure wasn't thinking about the end of camp or what will happen to all of us.

"I have been. I think we could make the distance work." She tightened her grip around me a little, almost like she was fighting the words for them to come out. "I really care about you, Dee. I do. I know we've known each other for such a short time, but you make me feel things I haven't felt before. I'm all bubbly like a soda with you."

"The feeling's mutual," I said, smiling softly. "And I guess Brighton and Belleville aren't *so* far apart. We could make it work."

"We can Skype all the time." She paused for a moment and I soaked in the silence. "And, we're not too far off from being able to get our own cars anyway."

"Those are expensive though," I said with a small sigh.

Long distance dating as a teenager is not a good idea. Just don't do it, friends. It sounds great on paper. The whole idea of waiting to be with that one special person because they were handmade for you. Newsflash. Nobody is handmade for you, and if one person was, another person is too. We have more than one soulmate. Don't put all your eggs in one basket. All that stuff. But I promise you, the story isn't over yet. I just... I just think things could have played out a little differently.

"They are." Jasmine sighed. "But we can make it work. And there's always camp next year."

"I haven't decided if I'm gonna come next year." I shrugged. "This isn't honestly my cup of tea. I love that I met you and Taron and Seth, and you guys are wonderful. But I just can't see myself wanting to spend another summer surrounded by bugs and the wilderness as an excuse to write stories. I can write stories from the comfort of my bedroom." I brushed some hair out of her face. "And I do really miss summer adventures with my school friends."

"I know. I do too. Well,"—she sighed—"Shelby is my only *real* friend. That's why I like coming here. Because I miss her over the year. She doesn't live in Brighton or even near me. I see her three times in the year if I'm lucky and that's because her parents drive her down to spend time with me over March break, the New Year's break, and usually one of the long weekends in October."

"Well, that sucks. Sorry you can't see her more."

"It's okay." Jasmine blew a soft raspberry. "I guess I just thought I'd have more going for me than being the poet girl that plays ukulele in the band room." She shrugged. "I suppose I have written myself as that character and it's too late to change."

"Not true," I told her. "It's never too late to change. You can still make a bunch of friends before college."

"Ah, see, *before* college?" She shook her head. "I'd rather wait till college and make friends with people in my program. At least that way we have some kind of basic common interest."

"Also smart."

"No more talking about the future. It's bumming me out."

"Well, you were the one who brought it up. I was happy watching you dance in the light of the fireflies, but then you wanted a slow dance." I paused for a moment to take in the sounds of distant crickets and the waves lapping at the shores of the lake. "And we're slow dancing to the music of nature, not even real music."

"Crickets are instruments too, Dee."

I scoffed. "They sure aren't."

"Well, they're their own instruments," Jasmine added.

"I guess they do play a good tune on the leg."

"So do I." She winked and clicked her tongue. The combination of close proximity and the moonlight gave me just enough brightness to be able to see her face semi-clearly. So that was nice, because her face was nice to look at.

"This is a perfect night," I whispered, a third to me, a third to Jasmine, and a third to the stars and the bugs and the trees.

Jasmine nodded and laid her head down on my chest as we slowly made our circling steps. "It's very nice, Dee. Thank you for asking me out."

"You're thanking me for asking you out?"

She nodded. "Yeah, because I low-key but very high-key wanted you to ask me out. I'm a little old-fashioned like that. I think the boy should ask." She smiled. "So thank you for asking."

"My pleasure," I said, pulling her body close to mine. It made moving awkward, but I didn't need to be moving; I didn't want to be moving. I just wanted to be *here*.

"Did you think I was gonna say no?" Her breath was warm on my chest. I could feel it through my shirt. Her cheek was warmer though. Her jaw rested back into place and she looked up in wait of my reply.

I sighed softly. "I mean, yes and no."

"Oh?"

"Well, yeah, I mean, I sort of figured you were gonna say yes. We had a connection, so I didn't *really* have a reason to think you'd say no."

"But?" she asked.

"But," I said, "there's always a margin for error, in everything, even sure things."

"You have a point." She looked up at me and smiled. "I just had an idea."

"Is it a good one?" I asked, trying to make my tone seem equal parts inquisitive and teasing.

"It might be. If you're athletic enough to pull it off with me?"

"Well, what is it?"

She smirked. "I was thinking we could steal some bikes from the camp sheds and ride into the nearest town one of these days." Her eyes lit up in the dark. She was loving this idea, the idea of running away together, the idea of a never-ending summer adventure, the idea of never having to return to reality. Even I loved the idea of living eternally in a hazy summer daydream.

"Won't we get in trouble?"

"For leaving camp? Oh, yeah, probably," she replied. "But just because it's a liability or whatever. Like, what if we got murdered or robbed or kidnapped? What if we get attacked by a bear? Oooh, insurance mess and phone calls and the camp would probably shut down in the aftermath because it can't keep track of the campers." She shrugged. "But we'll be fine. I have bear spray, and I'm sure Fred can protect us."

"I bet Fred can, but let's not get attacked by bears, okay?"

"No promises. If I see a bear, I've gotta at least *try* to give it a hug. Can't help myself. Especially the little cubs, they're so cute."

I sighed. "Okay, but I'm not staying around. You're on

your own if want to hug a bear."

"I want a bear hug from you," she said, a small smile stretching its way onto her face. It's like she set herself up to make that corny-ass joke.

"Here." I let go of her and she took a step back. "Are you ready? 'Cause I'm not gonna hold back. I'm gonna squeeze the life outta you."

"Give me your worst, Dee. I can handle it."

"Okay." I stepped up to her and wrapped my arms around her and lifted her up as I tightened my grip. She was all smiles, even though there's no way she could breathe properly. I put her down after a few seconds and she smiled at me.

She regained her balance and smiled. "I liked that. That was nice. Let's do it again sometime." She knelt down and fixed her shoe. I guess my bear hug had dislodged it. She stood up again and took a deep breath. "Huh, I guess you really took my breath away."

She's just setting up jokes, I thought to myself as I fell for her a little more with each one.

"Get it?" she asked, ribbing me. "Come on. At least pretend to be amused. It took me longer than I'd like to admit to come up with these."

"I sometimes spend hours coming up with jokes too." I smiled at her to let her know she was not alone in this. "I totally respect the hustle."

"I'm glad. Because spending five hours a day on coming up with quality jokes is a part of my life that just isn't going to change," Jasmine said. "And also Fred. He's a good friend. I'm thinking about moving to Ottawa with him for college."

"Oh, are you?"

"I am." She gave me a side glance. "You don't believe me?"

"Just hard to see you living in Ottawa all alone with a cabbage."

"You're a cabbage," she barked.

I faux-winced. "Ah, but I'm not named Fred."

"Change your name."

And we danced for a few more moments. And then the bugs were too much to handle. So we went and found somewhere nice to look at the stars and eat some trail mix. I don't like trail mix, but Jasmine does, so I just sort of put up with it.

And then I figured I should offer to walk her back to her dorm, which was just across the common room from my dorm hallway. But it was the principle of the thing, walking/driving the girl home after the first date. It may be a cliché, but it's a cliché I happened to enjoy very much. So don't ask me to not include it in my personal novels, 'cause I'm still gonna.

"You looked spaced out?" Jasmine said, finally breaking us out of crickets-and-wind silence.

"Sorry, I kinda am."

"What's on your mind?"

"This," I replied, "all of this."

"What about it?" Her eyes darted around my face. I could only tell because of the changing reflection of the moon in the spot where her eyes should be.

I shrugged softly, not letting go of her. "I guess I'm just soaking up the moment."

"I understand." She rested her head back on my chest and sighed. "We should get going. It's getting pretty late and kinda cold."

"Let me walk you back?" I asked, even though I was gonna walk her back regardless. As I mentioned, the two dorms were very close together, linked by a common room.

She nodded and stepped away from me, letting her hand trace its way down from my shoulders to my hand. She interlaced her fingers with mine and smiled. "You lead, and I'll follow."

I walked and she trailed three inches behind me, her hand tightly laced into mine. We made it to the dorms relatively quickly. We hadn't even gone very far, or we had somehow slow danced our way back.

"And just like that, the night was over and the sun was racing towards a new day," Jasmine said softly as we stepped into the yellow glow of the overhead lighting outside out dorm building.

"Poetic," I chimed as she looked up at me. Gnats were still fluttering around us. A spotty shadow was darting around her face from a moth that couldn't quite figure out how to land on the lightbulb above.

She shrugged. "I mean, to my credit, I *am* a poet."

"And you actually know it."

"I do."

"So this is it." I took a deep breath. "The end of our date."

"Well, don't say it like. You make it sounds like we'll never have another one."

"So there will be a second?"

She nodded. "Of course, Dee. I had a fun time tonight. I know we couldn't do much, but half the fun is with the people you're with and not what you're doing with them."

"I don't want summer to end."

She put her hand on my cheek. "We'll work these things out when we get to them. Don't crash the car before starting the engine, okay?"

"That's a good metaphor." I leaned down and held her gaze, my lips just hovering near hers, and we waited, for a second or for ever. Both seemed plausible. But then I inched closer and kissed her.

SEVENTEEN

My face was awash in red. I can guarantee that. I stepped into my room and sat on my bed with a wide smile across my face. Somehow, even though I didn't do much of anything tonight, my heart was pounding in my throat like I had just finished a marathon.

"There he is!" Taron shouted as him and Seth barrelled into my room. Within seconds, Taron was sitting on my chair and Seth was sitting on a wooden chair he had carried in from his room.

"Hello," I said, greeting them as soon as the wind from their entrance died down.

"How was it?" Seth asked.

"Right, 'cause you two totally didn't sneak a peek out the window or anything?" I sighed. "It was wonderful."

"Right."

"But," Seth added. "We need more details than that. Go on. Tell us everything. Tell us all the dirty intricacies."

"We met up and danced in the moonlight. That's it," I said. "Honestly. We just talked. I'm not gonna go over everything with you."

"Did you guys at all talk about what happens after the summer?" Taron asked.

"No. Didn't wanna think about the possibility of all of this ending," I replied. Which was so stupid, because had we just talked and decided to stay friends, maybe things wouldn't have ended so… weirdly? But summer romances are fun in that sense that the entire thing is just a daydream, an illusion you build up in hopes that the warmth of the summer sun stays long into the fall, but that's not what happens, no, not at all. (I can rhyme too!)

"Well, she lives in Brighton, right? That's not too far from you?" Seth said. I could hear the worry in his voice. He was so happy for me having been a part of Jasmine and Fred's adventures so far this summer, and now that the possibility of being together is real, I can see that he wouldn't want his friend to lose out on it.

But this is a story about falling in love.

And that's what I planned on doing.

"Yeah. I guess she's rather close to me. But we still don't have cars. We're just out of reach from each other, so we might as well be 500 miles away from each other."

Taron and Seth sighed and so Taron said, "But you won't be 500 miles apart, you'll be, like, 50. Relax. It can work."

"And then there's college, and that's even if we get into colleges nearby to one another." I let out a howling groan of desperation and defeat, and I let myself fall backwards onto the bed. "Life is hard, guys. Falling in love is hard."

"Well, I don't think anyone was assuming it would be easy," Taron said. "In the twenty-first century, everything is still harder than it probably needs to be."

"I've heard good things about Tinder," Seth noted. "Though that is a college app, so we're too young. But soon.

Soon I will have a world of pretty girls at my beck and call."

"Yeah, so if you make it to college, at least you have that option," Taron said, reluctantly admitting that Tinder was a viable dating option.

"I'm not gonna online date. At least, like, I don't think I will," I told them. I did. But that seems like a whole other can of beans that I don't feel like getting into. Maybe later on in the book, down the road some ways. Actually, I can probably sum it up pretty quickly.

Here goes: In my first few weeks at college, I went on several dates via dating apps and it was fun. I had a few hookups and it was good. Then I met a girl and we're together as I'm writing this actually. I bet sometimes you forget that I'm telling you a story and that the Dee narrating it is just an older Dee. I'm still me. But yeah, you'll meet this girlfriend later in the story, in the final act. I guess I'm telling you these things now so you don't just put the book down and live your life without knowing how the story of Jasmine and I ends.

"So you guys are just gonna, what? Coast along?" Seth asked.

I nodded and pushed myself back upright. "I suppose. I don't see what other choice we really have. I don't think we can be something *real*, or something serious, not yet anyway, but I think if we coast along, we have a real shot at being something real somewhere down the line."

"As long as you don't just give up on her, bud," Taron said. "So have you guys cemented a second date?"

"Yeah, we wanna do something as a second date, yes."

"Good." Taron smiled at me. "I'm real happy for you. You even look really happy and that makes me happy."

"Yeah, I remember when you showed up here," Seth said. "You looked kinda depressed, actually."

"Maybe I was a little. I guess I just didn't wanna be here," I said and then sighed. "But! You guys and Jasmine have made being here more than bearable, so thank you."

"Well, it's either I make friends with you or put up with

being alone with Seth all summer, and I don't know about you, but Seth gets annoying real quick," Taron teased, kicking Seth's leg lightly.

"Fuck you, bud," Seth snapped back. "At least I don't talk in my sleep and shout nonsense into the night."

"Nonsense." Taron scoffed. "This petty fool thinks my poetic midnight ramblings are nonsense."

"You're writing a comic series about clouds, whatever your ramblings are, I'm sure they're not poetic."

"Oh, and that's better than your sci-fi garbage?" Taron quipped. "What's it even about? What's it even called?"

"It's about the human race being enslaved by nanomachines they created to keep them young forever, and it's called *Ageless Tomorrow*, and you already knew about it," Seth replied. "At least I'm not trying to sound poetic. I know my book ain't poetic."

"I'm poetic," I added, just to throw them off their bickering. They bicker like this a lot. Usually about stupider stuff. Example: I watched them argue over which colour Skittle was better for 27 minutes once. Taron said red. Seth said yellow. They're both wrong. It's green.

"We know this," Seth said.

"Read us some of your poetry?" Taron asked, tossing me the small brown leather-bound book from my desk at me.

I cleared my throat and read:

What's a year to a week?
What's reality to make believe?
What's a spark to a flame?
What's a picture to a broken frame?
You handed me a pencil,
Erase me with your end.
You've always been good at that.
You've always been so good at that.

Taron nodded. "Okay, so that's pretty good. I liked it."

He reached over and took the book back. "So is this what you've been working on with Jasmine? Your poetry? I thought you got in for writing books."

"I did," I replied, "but why can't I also do poetry? Regardless of if it's good or not."

"I agree with Taron though, I like it," Seth stated.

"Thank you, friends."

"Poetry reading?" a voice asked.

We looked over to see Jasmine standing there in a bright blue onesie with flower buds all over it. I nodded. "Yeah, a little midnight reading."

"I just came by to drop off some more cookies." Jasmine handed a plastic container to Seth. "Goodnight, boys." She smiled at me and then walked away.

"I like her," Seth said, pulling the lid off the container. "She makes us cookies."

"What kind are they?" I asked.

Seth took a bite and grinned. "Lemon sugar cookies. My new favourite thing."

"She's perfected these into an art form," Taron said as he took a cookie from the container.

"I'm gonna convince her to open a bakery," I said, lying a little bit though. She only perfected this recipe because I helped her. It's not very hard to measure the same amount of stuff each time you make a new batch. Maybe *I* should open a bakery. Forget about this writing nonsense. I'm gonna get into culinary school and become a cake boss.

Seth sighed. "These are so good."

"Thanks," I said. "On her behalf, I mean." Except not really. Shh.

"I could picture you as bakers, the two of you," Taron stated.

I shrugged. "Maybe someday. Who knows. I do enjoy baking."

"And then you could give me free food."

"I'll give you a discount." I laughed softly. "But I knew

you just wanted the food. It's always about the food."

"Sue me," Taron said, tossing a cookie at me. "I just really enjoy myself some good discounted food."

EIGHTEEN

When the second "date" rolled around, I found myself asking why we were going on a date at quarter past noon, and why Jasmine requested such a specific time. Well, I found myself asking myself, not her. I don't question her about stuff like this. I usually just tell myself that she's a free spirit and that's good enough as an answer for now.

I dressed up casually. I knew Jasmine would be in a sundress, so I tried to find something light and not drab. I settled on a raglan tee and a pair of dark blue jeans. It's not much, but it'll work. Jasmine's seen me in much worse, so like, I'm not too worried.

"Good morning," Taron's cheerful voice rang into my room through my cracked door. Cracked as in it was a little bit open, not that there was a crack in the actual door.

"Good morning," I replied. "You can come in, I'm decent." I was buttoning the, like, four buttons on the shirt I had put on. Not sure why there's buttons, but they do look cool, but I also don't want my bare chest hanging out of my shirt. I'm not really about that life. I mean, I think I have a nice chest for a teenage dude. Toned but not muscular and also not entirely void of hair. You could tell I had hit puberty at least. Hit it hard, like a truck actually. I used to look like the biggest dweeb. I guess I do still, but the jawline game is stronger.

Taron stepped into my room and sat down on my desk chair. "So are you doing a thing with Jasmine today?"

I nodded. "We're supposed to be watching a movie together."

"Which one?"

"Not sure."

"Uh oh."

"She'll pick something good," I told him as I straightened my shirt out against myself. "She has, like, *really* good taste in everything."

"Except men," Taron quipped. He smirked at me. "No, I'd say you're a pretty good catch."

"I'd hope so." I sighed. "I know there's plenty of fish in the sea, but my ocean's a fishbowl, and she's the only goldfish for me."

"There are plenty of other fish, Dee." Taron tapped his head. "Don't confine yourself to a fishbowl when you could enjoy an entire ocean, yeah?"

"Well, it's not so bad with her," I told him. "I like her. She likes me."

"But we're still young."

I shrugged. "We can make it work if the love is real."

"I'm just saying." He gave me a small smile. "I know summer romances always feel so real in the moment, but what happens when the weather gets colder and we all have to go home back to our regular Monday-to-Friday lives?"

I groaned. "I'm trying to not worry about that. I just wanna have fun and make her fall in love with me. Love can conquer all distances, all boundaries. Love knows no limits."

"Sure it does," he said. "What about all those long-distance relationships that don't work exactly because of the distance?"

"Love has very far limits."

He nodded. "Far yet reachable limits."

"You're oddly pessimistic today," I said, walking over to him. I took his shoulders in my hands and stared him down. "Are you okay?"

He shrugged. "Yes. I'm just being real."

"Be real some other time."

"You're right." He sighed. "I guess you think about that all the time."

"About falling in love and then having it get all sorts of messed up because of distance and differing life paths?" I cocked an eyebrow. "Yes, Taron. Yes. I think about that all the time. Jasmine is a wonderful girl and I'd be lucky to share love with her for even a day, but if I get that love and then lose it, that'd kill me. Nobody likes to lose love."

"Do you think you'll lose her?"

I sighed and walked back over to my bed and sat down. "I don't know. I don't even *have* her yet."

"Good point. Do you think you should go meet her for your li'l movie date?"

I shrugged. "I guess I should, huh?"

"I mean, you don't have to if you don't want to."

"I want to." I nodded to the door. "Get out. Lemme mentally prepare for this."

"You're an idiot, Dee."

"But I own it." I winked at him. "Okay, get out of here." I straightened up my room. I had made a mess of my clothes trying to find something to wear. Every date is like this. I always aim to impress.

After a few moments, I stepped out of my room and stepped into the hallway. I shut my door and headed down into the common room. No Jasmine, at least not yet. But I wasn't too worried about it.

I sat down on the couch in front of the TV. The common room was empty. Probably because it was a nice day outside, so everybody was out and enjoying the sun and shade. Come to think of it, after this movie, I'm gonna convince Jasmine to go outside on a walk with me. I'd like to enjoy this nice day.

"Hello," Jasmine's voice echoed through my head.

I spun my head around to see her stepping into the common room from outside. I stood up. "Hello."

"Have you been waiting long?" She stepped up to me and we matched each other's gaze. She smelt like summertime. She took my hand and put it on her cheek. It was warm, sun-kissed warm. She smiled. "It's very nice outside." Her hand cupped my cheek. "Wanna go for a walk after our movie?"

"Let's watch the movie and see where it takes us."

"For a walk." She smirked. "It really is quite beautiful outside. What if I offer to hold your hand and give you an orange soda?"

"Well, now, that really sweetens the deal."

She smiled and walked over to the TV. "Okay, so did you decide on a movie? If not, I know what we're watching."

"Then what are we watching?"

She smiled. *"Ratatouille."*

"Ratatouille?" I asked. She nodded. And so I said, "Why?"

"Because I love this movie."

I smiled. "Okay. Put it on."

And so she did.

And we sat on the couch and watched this movie about a chef mouse. My favourite thing about watching movies with a girl I liked was that we got to do the whole "getting closer until we're just finally cuddling" thing. And Jasmine's "getting closer until we're just finally cuddling" game was very strong. She did the foot tapping and then the leg rubbing and the fingers touching and then eventually she was just laying up against me and my arm was around her. I was awash in the smell of her lavender-lilac-floral shampoo and the smell of the wild summertime air that was still lingering on her.

The movie credits started to roll and she got up. "Well, that was just as amazing as I remembered it. Now, our walk?"

I sighed, feeling the sudden absence of her warmth on my side. "Yes, our walk. You owe me an orange pop."

"Soda."

"Pop."

"Then you're not getting it."

"Then I won't go on a walk with you."

She scoffed. "Yeah, you would."

"You're right, I would. Let's get some orange *soda* and we can take that walk."

The beach seemed to be forever away in my mind, but it never takes very long to get to it. Especially not when you have an orange soda in one hand and the hand of the cutest girl in the other hand. Jasmine was all smiles as she strolled with me and sipped her soda.

"I hid a bag of stuff here earlier," Jasmine said, using her tongue to guide the straw of her soda into her mouth. Oh, how I wished to be that straw.

"A bag of stuff?" I asked. I cocked an eyebrow. "What kind of stuff?"

"Oh. You'll see."

"I don't know if I should trust you, Jasmine."

She shrugged. "I think you should. I haven't led you astray yet. And I gave you an orange soda. I'm very trustworthy."

"Where is the bag?" I asked.

She let go of my hand and ran off down the sandy beach. "It's up here. Follow me!" She looked back after a few seconds and noticed I hadn't started running with her. "Come on! Run with me! It's a nice day. Come on!"

I sighed and jogged beside her for a few minutes until we reached a secluded part of the beach. It was blocked from view from the fields by a big bunch of bushes that extended down some ways into the beach, forming a sort of half wall.

"Here we are." Jasmine walked to a bush and pulled a large black duffel bag from just inside of it. She dropped it by my feet. "I needed to hide the goods from the fuzz."

"What goods?"

"These." She opened the bag and dumped a bunch of brightly coloured plastic buckets and shovels onto the sand. "We're gonna build a castle."

"In the sand?"

"Yes," she said, "sandcastles are built in the sand. I'm very glad you're learning."

I laughed. I couldn't help but laugh at the *way* she said that to me. "How big are we making our castle?"

"As big as we can. I wanna be a princess for the day."

"You already are a princess," I told her.

She smiled. "Thank you, but don't you agree that a princess deserves a castle?"

I nodded. She was onto something there. Every true princess does deserve a castle, and a castle of sand is still a castle at the end of the day. So we go to work building a sandcastle. It was a sloppily made mess, but she was smiling when we were finished with it. "Ta-da!" she exclaimed, her arms outstretched. "I love it." She stepped inside the walls of this castle and looked at me. "I'm the princess of this castle now."

"You sure do seem awful lonely in there," I said. "Do you need a prince?"

"Maybe someday. For now, reach into the duffel bag and pull out an orange soda. The princess is thirsty. Building this sandcastle has got me parched."

I smiled and walked over to the duffel bag. I dug around and pulled out a can of soda. I tossed it over to her and she sat down inside the walls of the castle grounds and opened her drink.

She nodded for me to come sit next to her. "This was a nice day to do this, don't cha think?"

I nodded. "I do." I cracked open the soda I got for me. "Thanks for doing this with me."

"No problem." I smiled at her. "I had fun today."

"I really like you, Dee."

"I really like you too, Jasmine."

NINETEEN

The beach outgrew its welcome on us after a while. We began to feel the draw of the outside world again and as the sun began to slip down towards the horizon, we decided we'd better set our sails on a new adventure. That and we went to get food from the caf because we were hungry. We were walking, one hand on her, one hand on a hot dog.

"Where to now?" I asked.

Jasmine shrugged. "Anywhere."

"What if we just walk forever in one direction until we end up somewhere new?"

"Well," she said, "the only thing for miles and miles around us in any direction is more forest and hills and lakes and then—guess what's after that—more heckin' forest and hills and lakes."

I wished we could just walk off into the woods and end up somewhere, like that movie *Bridge to Terabithia* or something. Hell, I'd even settle for Narnia or a home for peculiar teenagers. The fun is in the adventure, right? Or maybe in strong hallucinogens. Either way, the forest has bears, so the bears would murder us. I tend to not go too deep into the forest for that reason. There was already a bear spotted near the camp a little while ago. It was shooed off by a park ranger, but still. Bears put a real damper on the whole adventure thing.

"Whatcha thinking about?" Jasmine asked.

"Bears," I replied vacantly.

"Bears?"

I nodded. "Bears."

"Why are you thinking about bears?"

"Well, the thought of walking through the forest is really cool and all, but then I thought about how there was that bear last week or whatever and then I was thinking about how bears terrify the living shit out of me and that I don't wanna ever be in the same space as one." I shrugged. "Bears put a damper on my forest adventure plans."

"We could always walk up the road. They have fences that keep bears off it."

"Maybe we could bike into the nearest town."

Jasmine's eyes lit up. "Hecking yes!"

"Yeah?" I laughed. "I knew you'd like the sound of that."

"I do."

"Hey." She stopped walking. "I have a thing I wanna do."

"Oh?"

"Follow me," she said, taking me to the side of the dirt trail we had been walking. We walked through the trees. I was careful not to get branch in my half-eaten hot dog.

"Why are you taking me into the trees?"

"You ask so many questions, Dee." She turned to me and pulled my face down and kissed me. "Just trust me. There are no bears here."

"Okay, okay, but why are we going into the woods?"

"There's a little clearing up here with a lonely tree," she replied. "And I want the tree to have some company."

"You want us to keep a tree company?"

Jasmine nodded. "Trees get lonely too."

The branches and bush cleared into a small clearing in the forest. There are a lot of little clearings like this in this forest. Just little areas of grass, not much more than twenty feet across in any direction. And in the middle was indeed a lonely tree. A tall maple whose trunk was still rather thin. It still stood tall enough that you enjoy the shade it cast down around it. Jasmine walked up and looked at it. "Sucks that this isn't an apple tree. I could go for an apple right now."

"I'm sure we could find an apple tree," I told her as I walked into the shade with her. We had left the duffel bag stuffed behind a cabin back when we had gotten food, but Jasmine and run in and grabbed her little purse. It was beige and covered in flower print.

She dug around in her purse and pulled out a small bag of Apple Chews. They were toffee covered taffy that tasted like the candy-coated apples you get at county fairs. "Want some?"

"Yes, I love Apple Chews." I stuck my hand out and she dropped some of the little candy balls into my hand. I haven't had Apple Chews in so long. I used to eat them all the time growing up. I stuck a few in my mouth and chewed. "This is good."

She smiled ate a couple. "They're very good." She dug around her purse some more and pulled out a small knife. "Don't worry. It's not for you."

"Then what is it for?"

"I wanna be cheesy and carve our initials into a tree." Jasmine looked over at me. "I mean, D + J = heart, right?"

I nodded. "That's right. That math seems to add up."

"Thanks. I had the boys in the lab run the numbers a few times with all the different variables at play, and we got the same result each time," she said, twirling the knife in her fingers. "The numbers are stable. This is a very safe calculation."

"Did they account for fluctuation over time?" I asked her as I watched her start to chip into the tree bark.

She nodded. "Of course. My team is the best in the biz."

"Now, I've heard that before. I wanna see the numbers you ran. I want the raw data!"

Jasmine stepped over to me and pulled me face down to hers. "You want the raw data?" She rolled her eyes. "Fine! Have it, then!" And then she kissed me. And I kissed her. And then she pulled away. "I'm gonna continue to carve this heart into the tree now."

"Are you gonna let me carve half of it?" I asked as she started rounding out the top of one half of the heart.

"Do you want to carve half of it?" she asked.

I shrugged. "Sure."

"Here." She handed me the knife and I went to work. "So have you thought about what comes after this summer for the two of us?"

"Of course. I'm always thinking about what happens next," I told her as I whittled away. "But I thought we were gonna not focus on that for right now."

"Yeah." She fumbled her fingers together. Nerves. "But it's hard not to think about how this will most likely end badly. Like, what if we get accepted to colleges that are nowhere near each other? Can a relationship like ours—like that—really be sustained by one summer?"

"I think so."

"Well, how do you think so?"

I shrugged. "I guess if you see a pot of gold at the end of a rainbow, you keep trying to reach the end of the rainbow, right? Like, sure, it might take you over rivers and mountains and through forests and whatever, but you *know* what's waiting for you." I shrugged again. "I think it's worth the wait when you know what you're waiting for."

"Maybe you're right."

"We can at least try."

She nodded. "Sorry. I just overthink sometimes."

"It's okay," I told her as I started to carve my initial and the plus sign. "We all overthink sometimes. But just because we'll have to do distance, doesn't mean the distance is gonna win. Besides, it's not about being with someone physically, it's about the love two hearts share."

"And all that love-quotes-over-a-sunset-photo B.S." Jasmine sighed softly. "I guess you do have a good point though."

"I do," I said, finishing up my half of our carving. "I had my guys in the lab go over all the numbers. It's risky, but it should work out in the end."

"And if it doesn't?"

I handed her the knife. "Then it won't be for a lack of trying." She took the knife from my hand. "If you never play the game, you never have a chance at winning, only losing."

She shrugged. "You're right. Anyway, I just like you a whole heaping bunch. You're so cute." She carved a J into the tree and then a small equals sign underneath. "There, now D + J really does equal a heart."

"It always did, I think."

She nodded. "Agreed." She put the knife back in her purse and ran her fingertips over the engraving. "I guess this makes you my boyfriend, hmm?"

"I guess it does," I said, walking up behind her and wrapping my arms around her. I kissed her neck and smiled as I looked up to the engraving in the tree. Somehow, even though the tree would one day either rot and die, be cut down for wood, or burn in a fire—the etching felt eternal, at least in the moment we etched it.

"Knot your threads with mine," Jasmine said softly.

"What for?"

"So we may never drift apart."

I smiled. "I think I can swing a little knotting."

"Good. Because I intend to earphone cable the shit out of us." She smiled and dug into her purse. "Want another orange soda?"

I sighed. "I'm gonna have a real bad cavity from being with you, aren't I?"

"But it's because I'm so sweet, right?" she asked. "Not because of all the sweets and sodas I feed you?"

I nodded. "It's such a nice day." I headed over to a patch of sunlit grass and lied down. The sky was a picturesque blue. The breeze was to die for. The air was warm without being too hot in the sunlight. The day was perfect. Jasmine laid her purse down next to me and plopped out beside me. Her eyes were fixated on the small white clouds floating high up above us.

Her hand reached over and her fingers interlaced around mine. "Today was a good day. I'm enjoying all of this."

I smiled at the sky. "Yeah. I am too." Today had started with a movie, then a sandcastle, then some food, and then a tree carving. And now, here we lie in the grass, looking up at a blue sky as the sun started to make its gradual curve towards the horizon for the night to come. The air was already starting to cool after having been baked in sunlight. Even though we were still in the sunlight, it felt cooler than earlier on the beach.

Every day of this summer has been so beautiful. Even when it's rained, it's been nice. The rains are never torrential or overbearing. They've been light, cooling, and refreshing. They never stay for too long, and they never come at bad times. We've always had a good warning before the rain came. And then the sunny days were wonderful. Bright blue skies, wispy clouds, cooling breezes through the trees. And of course the people here at the camp made the days even better. Everybody from the camp director to Jasmine lying next to me.

I think I might love it here.

TWENTY

The air was warm and still today. Not overbearingly hot, but the breeze was much less pronounced than in recent days, so that was a bummer. But I walking across a large field that was cooking in the midday sun. I saw three people close together. Taron, Jasmine, and Seth.

I set down my backpack and pulled out my little hardcover notebook. "Hello."

"Hello," Jasmine said.

"It's about time you showed up," Seth said, looking up from his notebook. "What took you so long?"

"Food," I replied as I took my seat on the warm grass with them. "How are you guys today?"

"Better now," Jasmine said with a small smile.

Taron shrugged. "It's been okay. My brain hurts because—get this—I'm actually using it for something creative for once."

I gasped. "Wow. Really?"

He nodded and pushed his notebook towards me. "I've been making a lot of progress in terms of story planning."

"And the artwork?" Seth asked, looking up from his notebook. He had his laptop out too. I guess he was getting into serious writing also.

Taron shrugged. "I doodle all the time. I'm not worried about illustrating the story. I just need to *write* the story. And look." Taron took the notebook back from me and leafed through a couple dozen pages. "This is all from today and last night. I've been so productive. This feels nice."

"Yeah, ew, you look happy," Seth teased. "I'm in a similar boat. Look." He turned his laptop and scrolled through many thousand words. "That's all been recent."

"I'm so jealous," I mumbled. "I've been so caught up in life that I haven't felt the need to live vicariously through stories I create."

"Same." Jasmine smiled. "Anyway, I've been doing poetry things." She handed me her notebook and I read over the poem she had most recently written.

We're moonlighting as lovers,
running around under covers.
Look at how the sky hovers,
all the stars we discovered.

"Look at the cars passing by."
Your kisses in infinite supply.
Your friend's house, your alibi.
Till the sunrise sings a lullaby.

Still moonlighting as lovers,
running around under covers.

She took it back from me and handed it to Seth to read next. And then to Taron and then she took it back and looked at all of us. "So?"

"I really loved it," I told her.

"Yes," Seth said, nodding. "It gave me a vivid memory of something I've never lived through, and honestly, I need more of that in my life."

"It's not your best," Taron stated. He shrugged. "I just like *Neon* a lot better."

"Oh. Pfft." Jasmine pushed Taron a little. "I like this one more than *Neon*."

"Anyway," Taron said, cutting her off. "How's your writing actually coming along, Dee?"

I shrugged." I supposed it's getting there. I've written a few chapters and stuff. I've been toying around more with poetry lately. I guess I just think there's something deeper I'm trying to get at, and novels aren't the best way to get these kind of emotions across. You know?"

Jasmine nodded. "I can't write novels. I wouldn't be able to have that kind of commitment."

"Oh," I said, raising an eyebrow, "so you have commitment issues?"

"To writing, jackass. Not to you." She pushed me playfully.

"For me, it's both, if we're being honest," Seth chimed in.

I rolled my eyes at him. "Do you know where they keep the keys to the canoe shed?" I asked the group. Though this question might seem random to them, I had a reason for asking.

The three of them stared at me. Jasmine spoke, "Um, why?"

"No real reason."

"You're lying."

"Wow, how could you tell?" Taron teased. He turned to me. "Are you trying to steal a canoe there, bud?"

"I might be." I closed my notebook. "What's it to ya if I am?"

"I might want in on it." He smirked at me. "I know you're not strong enough to lift a canoe by yourself, Dee."

125

"I'd like to think I am." I looked at my arms. Maybe I'm not the strongest person at the camp (or even in our little group of four, to be honest), but I'd like to think I could handle hauling a canoe into the water from the canoe shed.

"We'll see," Jasmine said. "There's a spare key for the canoe shed hidden in the blue birdhouse nearby."

"Why'd you let us hear that?" Taron ask. "Do you trust us that much? Cuz that might be a bad call."

"I trust you," Jasmine said. "And maybe I was lying." She grinned at Taron. "Maybe the key's in the *red* birdhouse."

"Birbhouse," Seth interjected.

"Yes, a birbhouse. A red birbhouse."

"I thought it was a blue one?" I asked.

"It is," Jasmine replied. "But maybe it's also the red one."

"You're confusing me," Taron groaned.

I sighed. "So the blue *birbhouse*, got it."

"Are you gonna tell me why you want into the canoe shed?" Jasmine asked me. She raised an eyebrow. "Or is this one of those surprises?"

"No. It's not for anything. I just... need it okay? Don't question me."

Jasmine gave me a look. A look that looked like she was trying to call me on my shit, but I wasn't about to tell her the idea I had hatched. She sighed. "Fine. I won't question you... for now."

"That's wise. I'm ironclad. I would never cave and tell you my master plan," I told her.

Jasmine scoffed. "Okay."

"Honestly," Taron started, "Dee hiding anything from Jasmine is because Jasmine is letting him do it. Dee is a big ol' softie for Jazz."

"Am not," I said.

"Are too," she argued.

To that, I said, "True." Well, maybe I'm caught up in a summer romance, so of course I'm softie. All melted like ice cream in this summer heat. I looked over to her and she smiled at me. And I smiled at her. And everything just felt *right* in the moment.

And I know it won't always feel right. Of course I knew that. But in the moments when it does feel right, you have to enjoy it. Even when you have your fears about what follows and what comes next and the most probably outcomes. You have to have hope that it'll stay right. And that you can enjoy it in the moment.

TWENTY-ONE

As days pass by, I take more and more notice of how much Jasmine has morphed my summer. All my writing has been mused by her. Is that even how you use that word? Can something be *mused*? I guess something can be amused. Anyway, the days flick by and I cross the little numbers in the corners of my calendar. I eat breakfast, I go to the writing workshops, I hang out with friends, and I spend all evening talking to (and kissing (like a lot (a lot, a lot)) Jasmine.

I had to buy more notebooks from the camp "store." I use that word loosely because their version of the store is to just tell them what we need and they subtract it from an "allowance" that was paid as part of our admission fee. Whatever "allowance" we don't use, gets refunded at the end. So that's helpful. I think they set it up this way because some kids need more supplies than others, but they never really know, so I guess it's unfair for *all* the kids here to pay for a few kids that need more stuff, i.e. sketchbooks and special pencils (like Taron and his comics).

I opened my notebook and leafed through the poems I had written. Honestly, when did I become such a dork, writing poetry all summer about some girl. But she's more than some girl, right? I mean, obviously. Why else would we be a couple? She's more than *just* some girl.

We might be missing our edges,
But we're still masterpieces.

I leafed through some more.

from way up this high,
the cities look
like neon spiderwebs.

from way down this low,
the cities look
like they pulse with our veins.

from a distance,
in an instance,
at every entrance,
reluctant persistence.

every youthful urgency,
alarms like emergency,
dopamine insurgency.
falling for all to see.

dancing in the light veins,
caught up in the gold rush.
dancing the night away,
the spiderwebs catch us.

That one might be one of my favourites. I just like the recklessness it purveys. I called it *Light Veins*. I think Jasmine wants to add it to her collection, with a credit to me as the author obviously. She seems to really vibe with some of my stuff, but maybe she's just narcissistic and knows a lot of it is inspired by her.

I tossed the notebook to the bed and sighed.

"You okay?" Taron asked, looking up from the floor.

I nodded. "I just wish I was better at words."

"You're pretty damn good at words."

I shrugged. "Arguable."

"Barely," Seth chimed in. He shut over the book he was reading. It was called {23:59} or something like that. I dunno. It's a signed copy though, so that was cool. "So when should I go distract Jazz?"

"Soon," I said. I pulled my backpack over to me. I had packed away candles, a lighter for the candles, some li'l sandwiches (ham, turkey, and chicken), and a blanket. "I think I have everything."

"Better hurry," Taron said, closing his sketchbook. "You're burning daylight." He stood up and looked outside. "Do you have bug spray?"

"Fuck," I muttered. "I don't."

"I'll meet you at the canoe shed," Taron said, walking out of the room. "Seth, you're on Jasmine duty."

"Got it." Seth stood up. "Dee. Might I go and collect her?"

I nodded. "Sure."

"What does she need?"

"Pants. Shoes. Sweater," I told him. "It gets cold at night, so better safe than sorry."

"I'll see to it that she meets you at the beach." He turned to leave and then swivelled back. "Which beach was it?"

"Beach D."

"The one with the fuck shack, got it."

I chuckled and nodded. "That's the one."

He eyed me over. "You, uh, you guys gonna, you know?"

I shook my head. "No. Just go distract her."

"Got it, chief." He took off out of my room, closing the door in a soft slam as he vanished. I was left alone in my thoughts again for the time being. I zipped my backpack closed and fixed my hair in the mirror. Not like my hair was fixable. It's generally short enough that it does what it wants unless I have a metric shit ton of gel or styling cream.

I waited a few minutes and then headed out to the canoe shed. I pulled down the birbhouse like she said and shook the key out of it. Taron was already waiting by the door for me. "Took you long enough," he chirped. "Here." He handed me a can of bug spray.

"Thanks." I slipped my bag off and stuck the can inside. "Well, here goes." I stuck the key into the doorknob. The knob was old and kind of rusty. It was also wobbly, which made me think that using a key was a formality. You could probably just lift the knob and turn it and it would open. My old side door used to do that. Kind of unsettling now that I give it some thought.

"This place doesn't look creepy at all," Taron muttered as we stepped into the dark shed. There was a garage style door on the side wall to get the canoe out, but it was only openable from the inside, hence why we needed the key to get in. There was no working light when I hit the light switch, so we were working in the dark tonight. The place was dusty and smelled like damp. The sun was setting behind us, its light filtered through the dust we kicked up by opening the door. Maybe we should just clean this damn place.

"Think we're gonna get murdered?" I asked, closing the door and pulling my phone out. I turned on the flashlight. "How much you wanna bet that most of these have holes in them?"

"I'm not betting against that."

"That's smart. You'd just be losing money."

Taron walked over to a canoe. "This one looks okay." He popped up on his tiptoes and looked inside the red canoe. It looked decently clean.

"I like it," I told him.

"But."

"But," I continued, "do you have this same model in blue?"

"Piss off," Taron said through a small laugh. "Help me get this thing free." We picked up the canoe (which was heavier but also lighter than I was expecting). We carried it over to the big sliding door and dropped it. I felt the dust swirl up around my ankles.

"Thank God I'm not allergic to dust," I groaned, wiping the air around my face.

Taron sneezed. "Yeah," he groaned. "Wish I could say the same." He grabbed the bottom handle of the door and tried pulling it up. "It's stuck."

"No, it's not," I told him. I walked over and unlatched it from the ground. "It was locked."

He sighed. "Shut up, Dee." He lifted the door and we carried the canoe out towards the sandy beach next to the shed. "Oh, look, the paddles are in the canoe already."

"Good," I said as we set the canoe down. I handed Taron the key. "Take this. Go lock up the door and shed. We'll put the canoe back later tonight."

He took the key and grinned slightly. "Well, have fun tonight. You know how to use this thing, right?" He kicked the canoe with his foot.

"I'm sure I can figure it out."

He rolled his eyes. "Good luck."

I watched his walk back into the shed and pull the door closed. I heard the latch on the other side snap into place. I waited for a few moments on the beach as the sun continued to set below the treeline. It was getting quite dark, which is what I needed it to be. I needed to paddle this canoe down the beaches without drawing too much attention to myself.

The sun dipped down low and the light faded and so I pushed the canoe into the water from the sandy beach. I paddled slowly down the beaches. It wasn't too hard to figure out, considering that there was zero current in this lake (thankfully). I paddled it up to the shoreline of the beach I was meeting Jasmine on and parked it in the sand. I walked over to the "entrance" of the beach, which was just a small clearing in the trees that separated the beach from the big field of the camp. I sat down on a stump and texted Seth. And then I waited.

I heard the distant tones of Jasmine's laughter in the distance, which made me perk up. Seth stopped her fifty metres from where I was sitting and said a goodbye and then pointed to me. Jasmine nodded and continued walking towards me as he turned and walked the opposite direction.

"Hello," she said, an upward inflection placed on the end of her "hello" as there usually was. She always sounded so upbeat and happy. God, she makes my heart twirl and fall down.

"Hi," I said, smiling widely. I couldn't help smiling. "You look really pretty."

"Well, thank you." She smiled and held her arm in her hand and did one of those little half twirls. "So why'd you drag me out here?"

"It's a nice night," I said, standing up and looking upwards at the great vastness of the star-dotted sky above us.

"Agreed."

"Come with me."

"Where we going?" she asked, taking my hand in hers without more than a second of thought.

I tugged her hand and pulled her along. "You trust me, so keep trusting me."

She sighed. "Okay. I guess I have to." We walked onto the beach and she saw the canoe and sighed again. "Is this why you wanted the key?"

I nodded. "It might be why, yes."

"You're cute." She smiled. "So I guess that means we're going out on a midnight paddle?"

I nodded again. "Two in a row. You're on fire."

"I do my best." She walked over to the canoe. "So did you move this over here all by your lonesome?"

"Taron helped me get it out of the shed," I replied, "while Seth was busy distracting you."

"I didn't need to be distracted. I was doodling in my room."

"Well, better safe than sorry."

She smiled. "What's in the bag?" She lifted my backpack out of the canoe and looked at me. "Hmm?"

"It's nothing too important." I eyed her as she slowly put it down, waiting for me to cave and just tell her what was inside. "Shall we get in?"

She nodded and helped me push the canoe back into the water and we hopped on in. She sat down facing me as I paddled us out into the lake. "This is kinda nice," she said, assumingly watching how the moonlight lit my face.

"It kinda is." I smiled softly, looking down at her. "I brought snacks." I sat down on the bench and pulled my backpack over. I unzipped it and pulled out two small bags of chips, the little sandwiches, and some fruit gummies. There was orange soda in the bag too (because of course there was).

"So what's the special occasion?" Jasmine asked as she ripped into a bag of chips.

I shrugged. "Nothing. Just wanted to go on a late-night canoe trip." I smiled at her. "Is that a problem?"

"Not really," she said. "But only because you're going on this canoe trip with me."

"Well, I wasn't gonna send you out on your own."

She smiled and ate a few chips. "These would be good with dip."

"But… they're dill pickle."

"Yeah," she said, shrugging, "and they would be good with dip. Dip enhances the flavour of *all* chips. Not just regular, unflavoured chips. Don't be a prude, Dee."

"I'm only a prude about pineapple on pizza," I told her. "Shit is *gross*."

"Pineapple on pizza?" She scoffed. "What kind of backwards-ass pageantry is that?"

"Exactly that."

She smiled. "You find new ways to amaze me and make me like you more and more every day, you know that, Dee?"

"Well," I said, "I do now."

"Mm, maybe I shouldn't have told you that." She took her hand and traced little circles along the little bench she was sitting on.

I could eat chips under the stars in the middle of a lake forever with Jasmine, I think. Everything just felt so peaceful and right. The sound of waves lapping at the canoe were relaxing. The boat didn't rock much. The water was very still. Just the fireflies dancing in the distance had any movement other than Jasmine and I. She rustled the bag of chips at me.

"You good?" she asked. "You kinda zoned out a little."

I smiled. "Just enjoying the night."

She let out a small sigh. "I am too. This is nice. Thank you, Dee." She turned her head to look out to the lake. "I have something planned for us tomorrow. All your mysteriousness got me into a mysterious mood also."

"Ooh, can I trust you?"

"Of course."

"And you're not gonna tell me what it is right now though, are you?"

She shook her head and turned back to me. "Of course not. What fun would that be? Just meet me at the entrance of the camp at eight."

"In the morning?!"

"Yes, silly."

"That's too early."

"Who's fault is that? I didn't know we were gonna be out late tonight." She smiled. "I'll bring you a coffee or something."

I sighed. "Okay, deal. What are we doing? What does it involve?"

She smirked. "Wouldn't you like to know."

I would have liked to know, but surprises are half the fun. What's life without a little mystery? What's life without getting a little lost? What's life without a little adventure?

TWENTY-TWO

The morning was disgustingly bright. I was disgustingly tired. Sleep glued my eyes closed and I was in that weird numbness of being conscious before being awake. My alarm was still going off as I sat up on the edge of my bed. My hand took its time reaching the clock and I hit the snooze button. I let myself fall back into the bed, wrapping the blanket back up around me as I did.

"Fucking eight A.M. on a Saturday," I muttered into the blanket. "Who does this girl think she is?" I stared at the alarm clock, waiting for these nine minutes to pass by so I could hit the snooze button again. This was becoming such problem for me in the mornings. I would just snooze my alarm all day if I could, just never leaving the warm comfort of my bed. Something about being half asleep really appeals to me, I think. But I knew that if I did that today, Jasmine would kill me, most likely. She's a sweet little thing until she gets angry. (I assume. I don't make her angry, and I don't plan on finding out.)

At 7:26 A.M., I got out of bed. At 7:26:01 A.M., I regretted every decision I had made in the last 24 hours. I should have gone to sleep earlier last night, but let's face it, Jasmine got up okay this morning and she was up just as late—if not later—as I was. I was still wearing my jeans from last night. Guess I was pretty tired last night after dragging that canoe back into the shed. I put on a shirt and lied back down on my bed. I was playing a dangerous game, and I knew it. I was seconds away from falling asleep when another alarm went off. I groaned, slapped the snooze button, and sat back up.

My head felt cloudy and numb and gross. I couldn't even feel my teeth. I was *that* kind of tired this morning. I should grab a coffee. If I don't, I might never make it out of the building. I headed into the common room and filled the coffeemaker with water. I made sure it had coffee in the filter, which it did. One of the counsellors usually fills it at night to make it in the morning. Not sure why he doesn't fill it with water at the same time though. Whatever.

I sat down on a nearby couch and waited for the water to boil and filter through. I grabbed a travel mug from the cabinet and some cream from the fridge and did up a coffee. I added in one spoonful of sugar and swirled. I took a sip and sighed in content. This coffee touched the soul.

I checked my phone for the time and realized it was already somehow 7:42. I should get going to the entrance of the camp. It was a ten-minute walk (well, it would be with me being this tired still). I snuck out the front door and shut it quietly. Something about this early morning adventure makes me wanna be sneaky, even though I don't need to be. I just *want* to be.

I sipped my coffee and took my sweet-ass time walking up the little dirt road to the entrance gate. Jasmine was already standing there with a backpack on, sipping out of a bright pink travel mug. Bet, right now, she's drinking tea. I stopped in front of her and her eyes fell on mine. She was sleepy. She still had sand in her eyes. She was just as tired as me. She was regretting her choice to wake up this early.

"Good morning," she said, her voice still low and raspy, full of sleep. "Coffee?"

I nodded. "Tea?"

She nodded. "Orange pekoe." She rubbed her eyes and yawned. "Are you ready?"

"Ready for what?"

She smiled. "There's that can-do attitude."

"I'm just asking."

"Follow me." Jasmine started off past the entrance, to the outside world. I haven't left this camp since I got here all those weeks ago. "I stole us a couple bikes." She leaned down and picked up a black mountain bike. "This one is yours."

"And that one's yours?" I asked, pointing to a red BMX bike.

She nodded. "I'm gonna do sick tricks and shit, boy. Just you watch, except you'll be too busy eating my dust."

"Those sound like fighting words."

"Well, we can't really race," she noted. "It wouldn't be fair to you since you don't even know where we're going."

I went to quip something back, but she was right. I didn't know where we were going, so in my luck, I would race the wrong way and get lost and mauled by a bear and then she would have to explain how I managed to get myself mauled by a bear. *Well, he's kind of an idiot.* Thanks for that defence, Future Jasmine.

"Think you can keep up?"

I nodded. I chugged back some coffee, not letting myself worry about how hot it was down my throat. I needed the caffeine right now or I was not going to make this bike ride. "How long is this bike ride gonna be?"

She shrugged. "Half hour. I already rode there and back last night after you went in."

"You rode through the forest in the dark by yourself for an hour?"

139

"Yes," Jasmine said, "and it was liberating. I had a flashlight and a rape whistle and a can of bear mace."

"Okay, so why'd we get up so early if the ride is so short?" I asked her. Because I'd be down for going back to sleep until noon and doing this ride then.

"Where's your sense of adventure?"

"It's still asleep," I quipped, "like we should be."

"If we had shared a bed, I would have been easily persuaded into staying in said bed," Jasmine said, smiling softly. "Anyway, up on your bike. It's past eight and we should be on our way." She rolled my bike to me, took my travel mug to put in her backpack, and then picked up her shiny red bike. "Let's go." I watched her swing her leg over the frame and start pedalling. I was quick to do the same because I didn't wanna be left behind.

The dirt roads were still dark from under the trees, but the early morning sun was slowly climbing into the sky, shining its golden hues over everything it could. The sky was blue through the leaves. I followed Jasmine's red bike, her bum bobbing back and forth as she stood up on the pedals and pedalled. I was struggling to keep up from my general tiredness, but keep up I did.

The road was flat, mostly. We pedalled for twenty minutes and Jasmine pulled over to the side of the road. "Wait here." I did as she asked and stopped my bike where she had dropped hers and waited for her. She re-emerged from the bush. "Come."

Again, listening to her, I followed her lead. I dropped my bike to the side of the dirt road and followed her into the bushes. They were still wet from the morning dew, which honestly felt a little refreshing after biking hard for twenty minutes.

"Why are we off our bikes?"

"Well, you were right about it being such a short ride. I wasn't just taking you out on a bike ride." She grinned at me. "You should have known I wouldn't tell you *all* my evil plans, right?" She eyed me down. "Or are you an idiot?"

"I am an idiot." I sighed. "Where are we going?" I swatted another branch out of the way. Jasmine was short enough that she could just duck a little and avoid these branches. I had to move them totally out of the way.

"Just up here." She hopped down a small ledge, must have been five feet or so. I followed her lead and jumped down after her. Jasmine swung her backpack off and dropped it on the ground, when I saw the ground, I noticed it was sandy where she stood. A beach. "Ta-da!" She smiled and took a deep breath. "This is my favourite lake in the whole world. It's small and quiet and nobody else comes here. She took off her shoes and socks and walked into the water. "Look how clear the water is." She looked down at her toes as she dug them into the wet sand.

"I can see." The water did nothing to obstruct the bright pink of her toenails. I took off my shoes and socks and walked into the water until the water lapped at the bottom of my jeans. "You should have told me to bring a bathing suit." I sighed. "I would have loved to go for a morning swim."

Jasmine, without a word, walked back to her backpack and pulled out a pair of red shorts with white flowers on them and handed them to me. "Do you *really* think I didn't think of that?"

I smiled. "I knew you did." I looked at her and she smiled.

She knelt down and pulled a neon yellow bathing suit from the backpack. "Turn around, pervert. I'll turn around too and we can get changed." She shooed me behind a bush and we changed. When we emerged from behind our bushes, I got lost for a few seconds staring at Jasmine. She smiled, walked over, and kissed me. "Did you forget you were allowed to touch me?" She put my hands on her hips. "I'm your girl, remember?"

My heart skipped a beat and I smiled. "Yeah, you are."

"Shall we swim?" She turned and walked into the water. I

watched as the waves lapped against her, creeping up her skin as she walked backwards into the water. She raised an arm as the water reached her waist and with a single finger signalled me to follow her into the blue.

My legs moved before I knew they were even moving. I felt the water hit my knees, then my waist. Soon enough, I was neck deep in the lake. Jasmine swam out a few feet from me and treaded water, waiting for me to do the same, I would assume, and so I did. I pushed off the sand on the bottom and floated out to her.

"Where to now?" I asked.

"Anywhere," she replied, diving under the water. I watched as her silhouette swam under the water a few dozen feet away from me. She emerged from the water and shook the wet hair from her face. "Come on out. It's not that deep. Don't be scared."

"I'm not scared." I swam out to her.

She wrapped her arms around my neck and pulled me close to her. The morning sunlight glittered off the water around us. The light of it dancing in her eyes. I smiled, because I couldn't help but soak in the beauty of the moment. The golden hues of her eyes lighting up with every wave crashing against us that flickered sunlight onto her face.

"You're beautiful," I told her, my voice low and soft.

She smiled. "Thanks. I could tell you were about to say something lame. I mean, it's cute and I really liked that you said it, but it's still lame in principle."

"I'm hungry."

"You can eat after we swim."

"Did you bring breakfast?"

She nodded. "Obviously." She slipped beneath the small waves and swam around me, resurfacing behind me. "Come swim with me."

I smiled at her and we swam laps around the small li'l lake. Then we splashed each other with water and tried catch a water snake. When we were done, we lied on the tiny little sand beach and she pulled her backpack over. The sun was now a lot higher in the sky and her skin was glistening in the sunlight. I guess mine was too. Water droplets tend to make things glisten, hmm?

"Here." She handed me a bagged PB&J sandwich. "You should eat up. We still have to finish our bike ride."

"This wasn't our entire day?" I asked, half joking as I took the sandwich from her.

She smiled. "No. We have more to do." She opened a bag and took a sandwich out and ate it in no more than five bites. I quickly ate my sandwich and then she forced us back behind our respective bushes to change back into our other clothes. She took our wet stuff and wrung them out as best she could before sticking them in a plastic bag and then putting the bag in her backpack.

She guided me back to the road where our bikes were still sat in the dirt, untouched and unmoved by any thefting bears. We picked them up and she turned to me. "Okay, you know the drill. Follow me."

I walked over and kissed her. "Got it, babe."

The rest of the ride went by quickly. We pulled to a stop in front of a small pizza shop in the nearest small town. Jasmine dropped her bike and smiled at me.

"Yes?" I asked her, acknowledging that she was staring at me.

"Are you hungry?" she asked.

"Not yet. We ate pretty recently."

She nodded. "Okay, we'll come back for pizza." She pulled out a bike lock and locked her bike to a nearby post. I rolled my bike over and she swung the long around both frames and then clicked the lock shut. "I hope I remember the combination later."

"Funny. I'm not walking all the way back to camp," I grumbled. "Biking was already enough work."

"Oh, shut up, Dee. I was just teasing." She put her backpack on her back and looked up to the morning sun. "My combination is your name."

"That's kind of cute."

"Come on." She tugged me by the hand and started walking up the sidewalk. "I wanna walk around. I love small towns."

This town couldn't be home to more than a thousand people. Half of them were probably just cottagers. More than half, to be honest. The town was situated on a bridge of land that separated two lakes. Black Lake and Megan's Lake. Who Megan is, I don't know. The town was essentially a handful of east-west roads with four north-south roads. Two of those right along the coast of each lake the town sat on. For whatever reason, the town seemed almost dusty. Kind of how old western towns looked in movies. Just a thin layer of sand and dirt over the roads.

After an hour or so of walking, Jasmine sat down at a bench along the road. Weird how small towns just have benches in seemingly random places. "Sit with me."

I sat down. "Are you tired of walking?"

"My feet hurt a little. It has been like an hour." She pointed in front of us. "Look at the view." And a view it was. This bench, perched atop a hill at the far reach of the town, overlooked Megan's Lake in the not-so-far distance, a vast sprawl of blue sparkling in the sunlight. Maybe there *was* a reason for this bench to be here. "I think this is my favourite bench in the entire world."

"Why?"

"Because of the view," she replied. "And because right now, in this moment, of all the moments in the world that I've been alive for, I'm right here. And of all the people I've ever felt and cared for, I'm here with the one I care for most." Jasmine smiled. "Of everywhere I could be and everyone I could be with, of every moment I could be living instead, I'm here in this one with you. And I wouldn't have it any other way."

"You're really cute." I leaned over and kissed her and she leaned back on me and rested her head on my shoulder. The world sort of fizzled out of focus around us. The only thing that existed was us, the bench, and the view. There were no distant cars, no bugs buzzing behind us in the grass, no wave sounds from the other lake nearby, no nothing.

This moment was perfect.

Jasmine reached over and pulled an orange soda from her backpack. "Sorry. I'm thirsty." She cracked it open and took a long drink. She set it down between our thighs and smiled at me. She kissed me with the sound of bubbles popping in her orange soda as the applause.

It was around two in the afternoon by the time we made it back to the pizza place. We ate and walked our way down to the beach because Jasmine wanted to swim again. Not like I was in argument of seeing her in a bikini again.

I sat at a picnic table and leafed through a notebook Jasmine had brought for me/us to read. It was full of drawings and poems she wrote when she was, as she put it, "Thirteen, learning about masturbation, and hung up on a boy that openly picked his nose in class. It's not my best work."

It was full of drawings about dinosaurs too, for whatever reason. Bad poems and doodles aside, it killed the time while Jasmine swam around. She walked over to me after a little while and sat down beside me. "Miss me?"

"I always miss you." I closed the notebook and kissed her cheek.

She looked over my shoulder. "Can we get ice cream before we head back to camp?"

"Duh."

She smiled. "Good, because that was the whole reason I wanted to come here. They have the best ice cream. They make it themselves too."

"Ooh, fancy."

"Yeah, yeah. Come on. Let's go."

"Are you gonna change first?" I asked as she started tugging on my arm.

She shook her head. "Ice cream, beach, working on my tan. Hello?"

"Fine." I stood up and headed over to the ice cream shack with her and we got an ice cream cone each. Orange swirl for her and moose tracks for me. We sat back at the picnic table and held hands as we ate our ice cream.

Before I knew it, it was time for us to head back home. The sun was lazily drifting down to the horizon and we were starting to get tired and bored of this little town. It was a fun day and the day was done. We got our bikes and rode back down the dirt roads until we arrived back at camp. We left the bikes at the entrance and kissed goodbye. I walked back to my room, covered in sweat and dirt with sand in my shoes from the beach. Jasmine went off to return the bikes from wherever she had got them from in the first place.

The dorms were nearly empty when I got in. Everybody was still at dinner while I slunk into my room. I shut my door and sat on my bed. I fell backwards into my blankets with a wide grin. Today was a wonderful day.

TWENTY-THREE

Taron had stopped by my room earlier in the evening, after I had got back in from my day out with Jasmine and after his dinner. He sat and asked what I was up to till Seth found him and convinced him to go spend the next seven hours playing video games in his room.

Now I was lying in bed, staring at the dark ceiling, watching the static swirl in my vision. Lack of light really makes you see weird things sometimes. I started hearing weird things too. It sounded almost like my window was being toyed with, like something was trying to wiggle the lock open from the outside.

I got off my bed and looked to my window. I couldn't see out of it, of course, I had a long curtain over my window. Was I about to be hazed? Do writer camps even do hazing? And if so, why wait so long? Why haze me now? Wasn't the clothes in the tree thing a hazing in itself?

Regardless, I toughed up and walked to the window and

tapped on it. The noise from outside stopped and I got more worried. If the noise stopped, it was definitely a person, right? I internally sighed and weighed my options. I could not bother the window and hope they fuck right off, or I could open the window and catch the culprit. I went with option B, because as a human I have this affinity for curiosity. I pulled the window open and moved the curtain out of the way.

"Hello," Jasmine said, smiling. I could tell she was smiling by the tone in her voice.

"What are doing here?" I asked quietly. I didn't wanna alert anyone to the fact Jasmine was hovering outside my window past curfew.

She stepped closer to the window. "I'm breaking you out of here."

"And why are you doing that?"

"I can't sleep." She put her hands on the windowsill. "So... do you wanna go on a late-night adventure with me?"

"How can I say no to a girl as pretty as you?"

She smirked. "You don't."

I closed the window over and dug my shoes out from under a pile of clothes. (I had to tear my room apart for clean underwear. I'm a bit behind on laundry.) I changed quick and emerged in the moonlight outside my room's window with Jasmine standing in from of me.

She leaned up and kiss me. "I missed you. Now let's go before someone sees us and makes us go back to bed."

We must have walked for twenty minutes across the field and to a small beach on the lake. She walked over to a small dock and lied down. I followed her lead. From here, there was nothing to obscure the view of the sky above. It was just us and the thousands upon thousands of stars dotting the night sky.

The crickets in the background chirped their melodies, their night song, and the world otherwise was quiet. Except the occasional piercing howl of a coyote (not a terribly scary animal, I mean, a coyote ain't no wolf).

"Did you bring a sweater?" I asked her.

"No, but it's not that cold though."

"Whatever you say."

"There are so many stars," she said, her voice shifting to low and soft.

"There are."

"It makes me feel so small."

"Or big. It makes me feel big. Like somehow, maybe I do matter, because out of all those stars, I'm living my life here. And there's only one me. And that *one* me exists here, and it's me."

"That was a little deep." She rolled her head over. "Have you thought about what we're doing after we go home from this camp?"

"We're going home," I told her. "Obviously."

"Don't be a smartass. I was asking a serious question."

I shrugged. "I'm not sure Jasmine. We still have to think about our schooling, right? Maybe we can go to the same city together or something. A big city, right, with lots of colleges and universities so that we can have a wider selection and we could both be happy."

Her hand reached over and grabbed mine. "And we could move into a little bachelor apartment on the fourteenth floor of some grubby-looking apartment building. We'll both have to take three buses to get to school and we'll have no A/C and exposed brick because the drywall has cracked and fallen off over the years."

"Is that something you want?" I asked, slightly horrified at the imagery she was putting into my head.

She laughed. "God, no. I know it's not gonna be that bad, but the idea of a small apartment where we could watch the sun rise in the morning would be very cute."

"Where we could drink tea on lazy Sunday mornings."

"And the sun would cast a golden light across everything, painting lines in the slats from out blinds."

"Where we could watch the dust float through the air in the sunlight."

She squeezed my hand. "In our pyjamas."

"And with a box of pancake mix on the counter so we can make breakfast."

"With blueberries or chocolate chips?"

I scoffed. "Like we wouldn't have both? Come on, use your head."

"True." She smiled at me. "Is this where I propose?" We exchanged a small laugh. "This won't just be a nighttime-talk dream, will it?"

"What do you mean?" I rolled my head to look at more intently. In the moonlight, I could see that she had put on a brave face, like she was fighting off *that* certain kind of sadness, the kind that comes with knowing the chance of this future happening is slim to none. I then realize that I was feeling the same kind of sadness, that I was holding it back and repressing it too.

She sighed softly. "Like, this is all fun and games to dream about, but I don't want it to just be something we forget. I wanna make this a reality. You're special, Dee. I like you so much it scares me sometimes."

"I mean, same. You're so perfect and you fit into my life outlook well. I dunno. It's hard though, right? We don't really know where our lives will take us. We're still so young."

"You're not supposed to talk logical to me. You're supposed to tell me that we'll figure it out, make it work. You want this too, right?" she asked. "The apartment? The sleepy mornings? The happy, perfect life?"

"I do. I just… don't wanna get our hopes up." I sighed softly and stared at the great expanse of space and wished it would just swallow me whole and murder me in the vacuum so I wouldn't have to think of the fact that eventually Jasmine and I would stop working as a couple, and then this dream of the apartment and the sleepy mornings would fizzle out. That one day, we would forget we had ever made these plans at all.

Her hand gripped mine a little tighter. "But that doesn't mean we can't have hope for it, right? We can still hope for the best."

"The higher our hopes, the harder the fall." I squeezed her hand back. "I'm not trying to undermine you or ruin our vision of the future, but I'm trying to be real with us *for* us." I took a second and breathed out. "I don't think building wild pipe dreams are gonna make any of this easier for us."

"But you want me, right?" Her voice cracked softly, subtly. It was subtle enough that maybe she didn't even know it had cracked.

I nodded and smiled. "Of course I do. I want you for as long as possible. But the reality is that we have a lot of deciding to do on our futures before we can figure out a future together. We can always look for schools in the same city, you know? But we still have to do that and get past that hurdle first."

"Ottawa?"

"Ottawa?"

She nodded.

"Why Ottawa?" I asked.

She shrugged. "Why not? Big city, but not too big. Safe, for the most part. Good schools. Lots to do. Good job opportunities."

"Did you do research on this?"

"For myself, yeah. So I know now that I've decided that I wanna go to Ottawa, but I'm open to other suggestions, of course."

"That's where Taron is from," I noted.

She nodded. "It is. But that's not why I wanna move there. In my defence, I had actually forgotten he lives there until you just reminded me."

"Well, where would you wanna go to school?"

"Um." She tapped her lips with her finger. "Haven't gotten that far."

"Goulbourn looks nice. They have a really good professional writing program."

"Oh, a *professional* writer."

I laughed softly. "Yeah, like copy-writing and technical writing, grants and proposals and stuff." I shrugged. "I guess I just really see myself writing, whether boring business-y shit like that, or fictional stories. I just like writing, you know? Words amaze me."

"You amaze me."

I smiled, maybe even blushed a little. "Thanks. You're pretty amazing yourself."

"You're just saying that cuz I said it first."

I scoffed. "No, I'm not."

She squeezed my hand and scooted herself closer to me. "I'm hungry."

"And what, you didn't bring a backpack full of snacks?" I asked. "You're usually more prepared than this."

"Usually. I wasn't in my room when I had the idea to come collect you for a night on the town." She sighed. "Okay. I got it. Get up. We're going for a walk."

TWENTY-FOUR

The bottoms of Jasmine's shoes were wet from the grass and coated in a thin layer of sand that had been pounded into the creases and crevices of the soles. I did my best to hold her foot in place as she tried to reach up for the window latch on the backside of the cafeteria. We were hidden in the dark and hidden from view, but this was still a delicate matter that required our precision sneaking skills.

"More to the left please," she groaned as she hopped down and stepped a few feet to the left. "I can't reach the stupid latch."

"Why don't you just have your keys with you?" I whined as I stepped over to her and put my hands back on my knee to help boost her up.

"Because I forgot. Look, we both understand that I'm supposed to be better than this, but I'm only human. I fuck up sometimes. This is one of those times." She grunted as she used my hands as a platform, filling my hand with freshly wet sand and dirt. "Besides, this is more fun than going in the back door."

"I guess." I held firm and lifted Jasmine as high up as I could. Honestly, I'm lucky she doesn't weight a lot or my back might have given out by now. "Have you almost got the window open? My hands hurt and my knees are gonna dislocate."

"Quit whining, you baby. You're strong and I believe in you."

"Thanks." I rolled my eyes, not that she could see, but it's the principle of the thing. "Can you hurry up? The bottom of your shoes are dirty and they're digging into my hands."

"Oh, hush. The dog poop makes a good cushion, doesn't it?"

"You better be joking."

"For your sake, I hope I am."

I groaned. "I hate you."

"Shut up. Lift me, like, three inches higher up, please and thanks."

I grunted and lifted her up as high as I possibly could. I heard her give a little grunt as she pulled down on something. Next thing I know, a small white knob came flying straight down at my face. She fell down as I let go of her and clutched my forehead. "Fuck!" I shouted.

She slapped a hand over my mouth and shushed me. "Are you okay?"

I pushed her hand away. "Yeah. God, that hurts. Is it bleeding?"

She moved my hands away and pulled her phone out. She used the flashlight on the front and got a good look at my forehead. She kissed her teeth with her tongue a few times. "It's, uh, it's not bad, but it looks like it might swell a little, but no blood" She put her phone back in her pocket. "Looks like I really rocked you one."

I kept rubbing at my forehead as I looked up to the window above us. "So, how do you wanna do this? I help you in and then you reached down and get my hands up to the window so I can climb in?"

"Umm." She was drawing a blank. She looked to the window and sighed. "I did not think about that. I guess we can try that. If not, I'll just open the back door for you. Even though this way is more *fun*."

"Come on." I offered my hands as her stepping stones and she smiled at me. I hoisted her up and she pushed the window open (now that the knob was on the ground).

She reached down from the window. "Come on. The window is hurting my tit." Her hand dangled just a foot above me.

"You have to pull me as I jump so you can, like, carry my momentum up further, okay? If not, I won't make it and it'll just pull you down and that'll hurt your ribs." I waited for her to nod in understanding. "Also, what are you standing on?"

Jasmine looked inside quickly. "Just a big ol' table."

"Is it sturdy enough?"

"Yes, Dee. Come on." She snapped her fingers at me. "Up we go."

"Yeah, yeah. Are you ready?" Once she nodded, I jumped up, grabbed her wrist, and in one fluid motion my other hand reached for the window's ledge. I managed to just get it (with her help) and I pulled myself up to the window and in. She shut the window behind me as I steadied myself. When I turned around, she had her hand raised up for a high five. I slapped her five because I'm a good boyfriend. "You're such a loser." I kissed her quick and got down from the table. It was much darker inside than it was outside. No moon to guide our way. Just the dim emergency exit signs hanging over the doors cast any light.

"Right. Snacks." She pulled her phone out for light. Night vision goggles would have been preferred, but I'll make do with phone lights.

I followed Jasmine out of the classroom we had broken into and down the hallway into the cafeteria. "Why didn't we just use the key, honestly? My head is still throbbing. Like, what was that knob made of?"

"Love," she said sweetly. "And nickel alloy, maybe."

"A nickel alloy containing love, do you think?"

"Ooh, if that hasn't been invented yet, we should do it."

"Did you hear that?" I asked, grabbing her by the wrist and stopping her in her tracks. There was a soft pitter-patter of rain outside. "Good thing we got inside when we did, huh?"

"You're telling me." She continued walking. "At least when we leave, getting out will be easier than getting in."

"And then we can run straight back to the dorms?"

"Of course. We wouldn't want my little sugar cube getting all wet and gross." She mimed a cry at me and added, "Boo-hoo."

"You would be the one whining about getting wet."

"Well, not around you." She clicked her tongue at me. We stopped walking and she opened up a door. "And here we are. *Cafétéria Chez la Camp Lindrick.*"

"Wow, you know French. That's so hot. I'm literally swooning right now." I put the back of my hand to my forehead and breathed out breathily to emphasize my point. She punched me in the stomach for my sass.

"What do you wanna make?" she asked, running her fingers along the edges of the tables as we walked towards the kitchen.

I shrugged. "What are you feeling?"

"Burgers."

"Really? At one in the morning, you want burgers?"

"Well, it's not like we can order a pizza." She turned to me with her eyes wide. "But! We could make one."

I smiled at her. "I'll make yours if you make mine."

She stuck her hand out and I shook it. "Deal," she said. And we kept walking into the kitchen. It was totally black in the kitchen save for the emergency exit sign in the corner of the room. But that's okay. Jasmine flicked on the lights.

"What are you doing?!" I nearly shouted. "Someone's gonna see the light!"

"No, they won't. There's no windows in the kitchen, just vents" She motioned around us. "See. We're fine, babe. Relax."

I groaned. "Fine. I just don't wanna get kicked out."

"You won't. The only expellable offences are getting caught having sex, doing drugs, or being in possession of drugs," she explained. "Basically, no drugs and don't get caught doing anything you wouldn't want you parents in the room for."

"Why's it taken this long for you to tell ne the expellable offences?"

"Because they're in the handbook, all the rules are. You know that handbook you got the first day of class that you probably stuffed into your backpack and haven't touched, looked, or thought about it since?"

"Touché."

"You should really read it."

"Why?" I asked, looking over the pizza oven for the on switch.

"Because," she said, walking over and turning a knob, roaring the oven to life, "you have to know the rules to break them."

"Breaking rules isn't usually my forte to begin with."

"It's okay. I have work to do with you yet." She opened the pizza oven and stuck her hand down on the stone. "So this is gonna take some time to heat up. While it's doing that"—she slams the pizza oven door closed—"shall we begin rolling some dough?"

"Yes."

"In the walk-in," she said, pointing over my shoulder. "Right-hand side, speed rack."

I walked in and grabbed two balls of dough. "These ones?"

She nodded. "That's the ones."

"How do you know where they are?"

"I worked in the kitchen a little last year. I decided against it this year because I wanted to focus more on my writing, not slaving over a hot grill and pizza oven, so…"

"You worked in a kitchen. I can't see you as a cook for some reason."

She walked over and lifted her hand. "See this scar. That's a burn from a hot pizza screen." I looked it over. There was a tiny indent in one of her fingers with a pink scar around it. No bigger than a centimeter or two, so I had never noticed.

"Popped the blister?"

She nodded. "Of course. But I have the battle scar to prove I worked in the kitchen. Though this place is pretty easy as far as kitchens go. It's not fast-paced, so like, we could take our time and be extra safe." She looked over her hand. "Though, I do think it adds to my *toughness* factor."

"Which is nonexistent," I quipped.

She slapped my stomach. "Stop. I'm tough." She took the two dough balls from me and set them out on a stainless steel table near the pizza oven. She handed me a rolling pin. "You roll mine, and I'll roll yours."

"Deal."

She pulled down a little metal bin of flour. "Use flour. It makes a world of difference when you're rolling the dough out. Then use your hands to stretch it out a little more."

"Thanks for the lesson. I'll just copy what you're doing."

She sighed. "I guess." She started rolling out the dough, first by flattening it out a little with her hands. I followed her lead until she had a perfectly round pizza dough and I had one that was a little wobbly looking on one half. She smiled at me. "Pretty good for your first pizza. Now pick it up and stretch it and give it some love."

Again, I follow her lead and spun the dough between my hands to "give it some love," as she put it. Once we had our dough thoroughly stretched, she grabbed two pizza screens and sprayed them with oil. "So where are the toppings at?" I asked.

She pointed counter with a lid. "Under there."

I reached over and pulled the lid up and latched it upright so it wouldn't close back down on us. There were quite a few toppings: sauce, cheese, pepperoni, bacon, sausage, ham, pineapple, olives, mixed peppers, and mushrooms. "Wow, lots to choose from."

"Do you have a hatred for any toppings?" Jasmine asked me as she opened the pizza oven and stuck her hand in it (to check if it's hot, I assumed).

I thought for a second. "Just pineapple, probably."

"Okay. I also don't like pineapple. So no pineapple, please."

"Y-you want... *extra* pineapple?"

She glared at me. "If a pineapple so much as grazes my pizza, I will murder you."

"I'm gonna bury one single chunk of pineapple underneath the cheese and let you try to find it."

"You're rude and I don't like you anymore."

"You still like me."

"Nope." She pouted at me. "I don't like you, or your cute lips, or your cute face, or your cute arms, or your cute butt. None of it."

I watched out of the corner of my eye as we dressed our pizzas. She was giving me lots of cheese, putting the cheese on top of all the toppings (sausage, bacon, and green olives). I rolled cheese into her crust so her pizza would have stuffed crust. I gave her bacon, pepperoni, sliced mushrooms, and ripped up spinach as her toppings. We stuck them in the oven and she hit a timer.

"And now we wait," she said, walking over and hopping up onto a stainless steel table. She sat there and kicked her feet back and forth as they dangled.

"How long?"

She shrugged. "I did *just* turn the oven on, so like, probably twenty minutes." She sighed and rolled her head back, her hair falling along her back. "Shoulda brought a card game or something to kill the time."

"What, my company isn't good enough for you?"

She scoffed and rolled her eyes. "Shut up. You know your company is my favourite company and that I love it."

"The feeling is mutual," I said, walking over and kissing her. "The light being on makes me feel like we're gonna get ourselves caught."

"This isn't the first time I've done this. We'll be fine." She lolled her head back again. "There's no security. There's no boogeymen. We'll be fine."

"What if there is a boogeyman? What then?"

"Then he kills us and it's game over for us. Boo-hoo, that's how life goes sometimes." She smiled at me. "It's cute when you get all worked up and paranoid about getting into trouble."

"It's because I don't like the idea of being thrown out of camp and/or charged with breaking and entering."

"You won't be charged or thrown out," she said, then paused for a second before adding, "Well, probably not any-way."

"Wow. You give me a lot of confidence when you follow up your statements with ambiguity."

"Wow," she said, mocking me. "You sure sound smart using all those big-boy words." She stuck her tongue out at me and grinned.

"How much longer for our pizza?" I whined. I was getting hungry for this midnight snack. Midnight snacks are usually the best kind. The most satiating kind of snack.

She walked over to the pizza oven and pulled the door open. "Couple more minutes. The oven takes forever to heat up to begin with. It's still pretty cold." She walked back to me and pulled a deck of cards from her pocket. "Here. I brought these so we could play Crazy Eights, since I knew you were gonna get bored with nothing but my company."

"I'm not bored per se."

"Unenthused?"

"No."

"What would you call it, then?"

I shrugged. "The word doesn't exist."

She scoffed. "Whatever you say." She sighed and looked to me with annoyance in her eyes. "I hope it stopped raining by now. I wanna look at the stars."

"They still don't shine as brightly as you."

"Aww, lame."

I smiled softly. "Depends on your perspective." She smiled back at me and we waited for a few more minutes in relative silence as the pizzas cooked. She pulled them out and put them in pizza boxes.

"How many slices do you want yours in?"

I shrugged. "Six or eight?"

"Eight it is. It's easier."

"Is it?"

"You cut in half," she said, slicing my pizza into two half circles. "Then quarter." She sliced again, making four slices. "Then two cross cuts." Slice. Slice. "Then you have eight. Which is easier than doing the math required to cut a pizza into six equal slices."

"I didn't realize there was any math involved with cutting a pizza."

"Obviously, you haven't cut enough pizzas."

I scoffed at her. "Well, I would hate to have to cut pizzas for a living. That and I would hate being covered in flour every day."

"Here." She hands me a pizza box. "Let's go to the beach and have a snack."

The beach was so quiet at night. It always was. Jasmine sat down on a seemingly random place in the sand until I noticed that there was a small blanket laid out, like she had pre-planned our whole date. And I betted that was the case.

Maybe she even somehow knew it would be done raining by the time we were ready to sit on the beach.

"It's wet." Jasmine whined.

I laughed softly. "Yeah. It's fine though. We can deal with a damp blanket."

She smiled and nodded, sitting down with her pizza. "A perfect view." I sat down next to her. She crossed her legs and opened her pizza box. "Perfect for a midnight snack."

"It has to be at least almost sunrise," I told her. "But I suppose it wouldn't be so bad watching the sunrise with you."

She smiled. "You're on to my master plan."

"Or is it *my* master plan." I cocked an eyebrow and gave a small ominous laugh.

"You wish it was yours," she said, taking a large bite from a slice of pizza.

"Mine wouldn't involve watching the sunrise on a Sunday night before class." I smirked softly. "I'm just saying I wound have planned this better."

"Well, maybe next time I'll let you." She smiled softly, watching me fold a slice of pizza in half and take a massive bite. Sue a guy, I was hungry. "Could you maybe chew your food?"

"Why? I'm pretty sure you know CPR, so if I die, you can just save me."

"Well, I didn't take any Hippocratic oaths, so I might not."

I laughed softly. "Well, fuck me I guess."

TWENTY-FIVE

The morning came too quickly. And my sleep was far too short. I slapped my alarm to make the piercing alarm noise stop for nine minutes. It's 9:30. I hadn't gotten back into my bed until nearly 6 AM. That's not nearly enough sleep.

"Morning, sunshine," Taron shouted at me.

I mumbled incoherently and stifled a yawn. I swung my legs over the edge of the bed and rubbed my eyes. "Good morning."

"Fun night?"

I nodded. "I guess one could say that."

"Long night?"

"Most definitely." I gave a soft chuckle. I could live a thousand nights with Jasmine and I don't think any of them would be long enough. I could spend forever doing nothing with her, just sitting under the stars, interlocking our legs and our fingers, kissing each other's cheeks and foreheads. I think I could spend forever doing that.

"I'm assuming you were up all night with Jasmine, huh?"

I nodded again.

"Hopefully she looks a little better than you do right now."

I laughed softly. "Well, of course. She always does."

"Seth is waiting in the cafeteria, by the way. He saved you some breakfast."

"Well." I rolled my eyes and forced myself to stand. "I guess I could eat."

Taron nodded impatiently. "Let's get a move on then."

The cafeteria was full of kids milling about. My legs felt weak from the night before. Almost like they were made of gelatin, not flesh and bone. I could also barely feel my teeth, which is weird, I know. But the whole world was weird when I'm so tired.

Seth was sitting alone at a table. "Hello." His voice full of energy.

"Good morning." I turned to see Taron already walking off to his own class. Pfft, I guess Seth and I didn't want him to stay and chat anyway. Rude.

"How'd you sleep?" he asked me.

"I didn't."

"I know."

"How do you know?" I gazed down to my plate. A few strips of bacon. Over easy eggs. Hash browns. Basically, the same thing I've been eating every morning for the past two months.

Seth looked at me quietly for a moment. "I heard you thudding into your room this morning."

"Because you also didn't get any sleep?"

He nodded. "Up late writing. For once."

"Wow. Someone was productive. That's a new one."

He faked a laugh. "I feel like I haven't done enough writing this summer. Which is dumb since we're at a *writing* camp after all."

164

"Creativity just comes at weird times."

Seth shrugged. "Well, you better eat up before that gets cold." He forks some hash browns into his mouth and chews silently, looking off out a nearby window. Seemed like a lot on his mind today for some reason.

I started eating and watched him as he picked at his eggs. "You seemed really bothered. You okay?"

"I suppose I *am* bothered."

"What for?"

With a roll of the eyes, he said, "I guess I'm second-guessing writing as a passion."

I nearly spat out my food. "What? Really? Why?"

"I just— I can never do it. I've written maybe a few thousand words all summer. And that's if I'm being generous with myself."

"It'll come back to you. We all get into ruts."

"It's not a rut if it's forever." He sat back in his chair and frowned softly. "I dunno. Maybe it's not for me anymore."

"Well, what do you wanna do instead?"

His eyes met mine and then darted back to the window. "Who knows. Writing just doesn't feel fun to me anymore. Maybe I spent too much time throwing a ball around in the sun and it fried all my creativity and now there's nothing left in there but self-criticizing hatred for my book."

"Hey."

"Hey."

My hand stretched out to his. "If you feel like this isn't for you, then it isn't for you. Don't force yourself to do this or you'll never love it. Writing has to come from the heart, from the soul. Writing has to be a need because it's a desire, the same as eating good food or having sex. Writing, like those things, should never be forced if your mind or body doesn't want it."

"So, what am I supposed to do now? I don't have any other hobbies or interests. Writing has been my life since I was little, and now I have to turn my back on it?" Seth asked.

He kept picking at his food, not eating more than a half a fork's worth with each bite he did take.

I shrugged. "I don't know. I guess that's for you to figure out. What were you gonna take in college?"

"Probably business or something basic." He sighed. "Accounting. I guess if I'm gonna hate my job regardless, it might as well make me enough money to live comfortably in the middle class."

"Um, yeah. That's the spirit."

"I mean, there's nothing else that I care about."

"Well, at least finish this book. It's your first full novel, right?"

Seth nodded. "Yeah. And a dozen useless short stories."

"Short stories can be good for something."

"Like?"

I shrugged. "Collections?"

"I guess." He rolled his eyes and lazily stuffed some food into his mouth. "I'm just not feeling inspired."

"We should get to class though."

"We should."

"And then after class, we can reconvene in the common area to hang?"

He nodded. "Sounds like a good plan to me."

Class was boring as usual. I kept an eye on Seth most of the time. He seemed very uninterested in being here now. I wonder what had gotten him to the point where he thought he didn't want to write anymore. The things I've seen him write have been very good, for the most part. Could just be a rough patch. I'd be lying if I said I hadn't had a couple of those too.

Jasmine and Taron were waiting after classes for us outside by the baseball diamond. I wondered if anybody's ever been able to get enough people together to play a proper game of baseball. Probably not.

"Hello, slowpokes," Jasmine chirped as we walked over and took a seat next to them. Seth tossed his bag down to the side and lies back to stare at the clouds.

"How was class?" I asked, kissing her cheek.

"Boring." Taron butted in. "We're all too busy thinking about the campfire tonight."

"Campfire?" Seth sat back upright. "There's a campfire tonight? Why wasn't I told about this?"

"You were."

"We all were. At the assembly and last week. And scheduled campfires are on the calendar," Jasmine told him.

Seth shrugged and lied back down. "I guess I just need to develop my listening skills."

"Seconded," Taron said.

Jasmine grabbed my hand. "So we're gonna go to the campfire tonight right? You're not gonna bail or anything?"

I shook my head. "No, of course not. Especially not if you're coming *with* me."

"I'm excited." Jasmine squeezed my hand.

"Can we sneak in a few beers?" Seth asked.

I laughed softly. "And where would we even get alcohol?"

"Drone delivery." Seth sighed. "Do we get to make s'mores at least?"

"Would it even be a campfire without some mores?" Taron asked. "How can you have a campfire at a summer camp without s'mores?"

"You can't," I stated. "At that point, it's just a fire, and fires are arson, which is illegal, so therefore, campfires without s'mores are illegal. Thanks for coming to my TED talk."

Jasmine and Taron shared a laugh while Seth rolled his eyes. Not everybody can appreciate my comedic genius. And that's okay that Seth was out of the loop on this one.

TWENTY-SIX

As soon as the sun set, the bugs came out in droves. They always do. Summertime is the worst season by far. I hated bugs with a passion. My legs and arms and neck got eaten alive nightly. I swear. But the sky was dark blue and the camp staff had place little lanterns guiding us all out to the beach for the big campfire tonight. All we had to do now was gather our group and then make it to the beach.

"All I'm saying is that I don't wanna get eaten alive!" Seth mumbled at Taron.

"And all I'm saying is you're a weirdo for wearing jeans to a beach campfire."

"Bugs!"

"Weirdo!"

"Boys," Jasmine butted in. "Relax. It'll be like twenty degrees, max. He's fine in pants. You're fine in your gross floral beach shorts."

Taron scoffed. "Okay, but I still think it's weird."

"Maybe he's just embarrassed for you that you have chicken legs and his legs would embarrass yours," I said with a small shrug. "It's a possibility."

"Like hell it is!" Taron said. He picked up his bag of s'mores supplies. "Let's get going. I don't wanna be late and have to sit in the sand. I want a good stump." He was of course referring to a tree stump that had been fashioned into a seat near the campfire pit, of which there are more than a dozen stumps to sit on.

"You're a baby," Jasmine said as she screws the lid on her water bottle. It was holding some kinda of fruit juice mixture, orange and fruit punch I think. "Let's get down there then."

"Did somebody remember bug spray?" Seth asked.

"I have it," Jasmine told him as we she started pushing us towards the door of the common area. She got eager all of a sudden. "Do you think they'll let us stoke the fire?"

"I wouldn't let you anywhere near the fire," I told her.

"I'm not that clumsy or unsafe!" she protested. "I've set countless fires throughout my time camping here and with my family."

"And you're not doing it tonight," Taron said.

"Aren't you best friends with the owner's daughter anyway?" Seth asked. "I'm sure they would let you do whatever you wanted to the fire."

"Except put it out," Jasmine said. "Cuz nobody wants that."

Seth shrugged. "Except people scared of fire."

"Who do you know that's scared of fire?"

"My ex was," he replied.

"The smoker?" Taron asked.

Seth nodded. "Ironic, isn't it?" He stumbled over a small rock on the path and cursed under his breath as we shared a small giggle. The laughter earned us a glare from Seth.

The campfire was already roaring when we got there. Some of the other kids were sitting down and a few other were tossing a glow-in-the-dark baseball around. Seth ran over almost immediately to join in. Something about playing catch really inspired him to move.

"Care to sit with me?" Jasmine asked, noticing a stump just big enough for both of us to sit down on.

Taron set his bag down next to me. "Will you guys watch the snacks if I go join Seth?"

Jasmine and I both nodded and watched as he ran off to join the game of catch. I'm not sure it's much of a game since there's not really a point to it, but it's a good time-waster, that's for sure.

Jasmine grabbed my hand and smiled at me. "We have to find sticks for our marshmallows! How could we forget to get sticks?"

"Put that on Taron, not me."

"Good idea. It was his fault. He was supposed to get our supplies for s'mores."

I looked over and Taron and Seth throwing the ball around. "He remembered most of the things. Let's go find some classic branches for our sticks."

"Gross."

"Okay, you can go back and get one of the metal sticks."

Jasmine pouted. "No, it's fine. I'll use a gross branch."

"That's what I thought." I took her hand and picked up Taron's bag. I couldn't just leave it there when he had asked me so nicely to watch it for him. I swung it over my bag and let Jasmine lead me into a nearby bush for scavenging.

"Where do you think we can find the best sticks?"

"The woods." I nodded towards the thicket of trees.

She sighed. "Okay, but if I'm itchy from bugs or poison ivy, I'll personally hurt you."

I laughed and pushed her lightly forward. "Yeah. I'm so scared of you."

Jasmine kicked my shin softly as she started pulling branches down. "How are we supposed to clean these?" She picked up a long stick and looked it over. "I don't wanna jam mud inside my s'mores."

"You wet it and stick it over the flames." I shrugged. "Do you have soap? Disinfectant maybe?"

She blew a raspberry at me. "Don't patronize me."

"I'm not."

"Sounds like it," she said, handing me the first stick she had picked up. "This one's good enough. Only need three more."

"Three more, however will we find three sticks in a huge forest of trees that are full of long sticks."

"Enough of your sarcasm," she said, slapping my arm. "Here." She picked up a second stick. "This one looks like it'll be a good roasting stick too."

I took the stick from her and chewed my lip a little. Something had been nagging at me. "Jasmine."

She perked up and turned to me. "What's up?"

"Do you think we'll always be this simple?"

She laughed. "Of course not." She turned back to the tree branches. "People are not simple, Dee, by our very natures we are complex webs of insecurity and confusion. Just a monkey with anxiety, really."

"I didn't mean like that."

Her voice gets more serious when she said, "I know what you meant."

"Then don't dodge it."

"It's not something we need to talk about." She turned back to me and then back to the branches. "If you let yourself become consumed in a thought, then that thought is all you think about. And then it comes true."

"But if we don't talk about it, we can't avoid it." I grabbed her arm and pulled her around to me. "Why don't you want to talk about it?"

"Because!" She stepped back quickly. "Because it's not a good thought. It's not something I want to think about. We just have to get through another year before college, but a lot can change in a year, and what if we don't end up in the same place?"

"And that's why you don't wanna talk about it?"

"Yeah! Because you'll go back home and realize that putting in effort for me is too much work and then that's it for us. The distance will kill us. It's a cloud of suffocating poison. And when it comes down to it, I'm always the one that gets forgotten about."

"I would never."

"That's what the last boy said, and the one before that, and all the friends that have ever left me." Jasmine's eyes caught the moonlight and reflected the glossy waves of tear-filled eyelids. "It just sucks, Dee, because I'm the one who gets forgotten about. Nothing about me makes someone want to stay. I'm only interesting because I do weird things sometimes. And then when someone or something better comes along, BOOM, I'm left behind. Just like that."

"Jasmine," I said, taking her hand. "I'm not going to forget you or leave you behind."

"No, they all do. I don't even have any friends to distract me from being lonely. I would just wanna come home and talk to you, but you have a life and friends and I'll be too clingy or something and you'll leave. We won't make it through the fall let alone the year!"

"We'll still be chill in the fall," I told her. "And next year. And when we move for college. I have a good feeling about us, but we just have to figure this shit out." I squeezed her hand and looked her in the eye. "Together."

"You promise?"

I nodded. "Of course I promise, Jasmine. We can make this work."

She nodded back and smiled softly. "I'm gonna keep looking for sticks now."

I let her go and watched her scan the branches for another five minutes or so. My mind raced with the endless possibilities that we might not work out and the ones where we do work out. And how, and why, and when, and the millions and millions of ways this could go.

She came back over to me when she had found two more suitable sticks and whisked me back to the stump. I set down Taron's bag and Jasmine sat next to me. She was whittling the ends of the sticks with a small knife (that I didn't know she had) and made the blunt ends a little better for skewering marshmallows.

"Roasting sticks?" Taron popped up behind us rather quickly. He grabbed the first stick Jasmine had fixed for us. He eyed it over. "Good job on this one."

"Thanks," Jasmine said, focused on the next one.

Taron sat down on a nearby stump and Seth soon joined him there. We all got our sticks and our stuff for s'mores ready. We spent a good two hours singing campfire songs and making roasted marshmallows and s'mores. We laughed and sang and danced a little. I think every kid at camp came out for the fire too, so it was a lively event after all.

The fire begun to die out and people started to head back to the cabins. Though, our little group, which had grown to include Shelby, was still at the fire. At least we all had front row seats by the time we started getting bored of it. Taron then stood up and turned to Jasmine. "Can I steal your boyfriend?"

Jasmine gave him a harsh glare. "Bring him back in one piece."

"No promises."

I laughed a little. "I'll be okay."

She eyed me over. "Mm-hmm."

Once Taron and I got some distance away from the rest of the campfire, I guided the two of us down a desolate walking trail in the woods. "So what's up?"

"Have you talked to Jasmine yet?"

I rolled my eyes. "About after camp?"

He nodded. "About after camp."

"Not really."

"Why not?"

"She won't discuss plans. She's just scared I'll abandon her or forget about her or something."

"Girls are weird like that sometimes," Taron noted. "But she has to realize you guys won't make it anywhere without a plan in place, right? This isn't something you should just wing it on."

"I tried to say that we need a plan, but she's still stuck on us not working out. She's scared of that, so she'd rather just enjoy the moments as they happen and worry about the problems when they come up."

Taron huffed. "The problems can be avoided though."

"Yeah, *I* know that."

"But she doesn't think they can be?"

I stumbled over a branch and Taron caught me mid-fall. "Thank you." I straightened myself up. "And no. I don't think she thinks they can be avoided. She has that mindset that bad things will inherently happen to her."

"Bad things happen to everyone," Taron grumbled. "I just— This is so frustrating for me. You guys seem like you have a shot at having that something everybody wants, and she'll let it slip away so easily because she's scared of a little struggle? A little stress? It'd be worth it all in the end when the two of you end up happy and living together and then ten years later you can laugh about how stupid it was to be insecure about all of this."

The path went down a small hill and deeper into the woods now. Taron nudged me to go the opposite route and closer to the fields near the cabin. But maybe I just wanted to get lost in the woods instead. If I never had to go back home, summer wouldn't have to end. Jasmine and I wouldn't have to end.

"This just sucks." I swatted mosquitoes off my arms as we batted away a few low-hanging branches.

"I know it does," Taron said. "I just wish there was more I could do for you."

"You're a friend," I told him. "What more do I need from you?" We shared a small smile. "Besides, she wants to go to Ottawa for school. I'm sure I could find a way to move there for school as well and then it'd work out for us."

Taron nodded. "I suppose at least one of you needs to have the long-term goal figured out." He laughed a little. "Maybe that's why she doesn't wanna make a plan, because you already have so many figured out."

I shrugged as we entered the field from the woods. "Maybe that is why."

"I figure you might as well think of it like that to save yourself from being consumed by the thought that she doesn't want the same future you want."

I cocked an eyebrow at him. "That was *not* a thought I had until you just mentioned it right there, so thanks for that one."

"Ah, shit. I'm sorry. Forget I mentioned that."

"Lemme just hit the control-alt-delete combo in my brain real quick."

Taron stayed quiet as we walked back to the cabin. It took us a lot longer to walk the field than I imagined.

"Dee," he piped up finally.

"Yes, Taron?"

"I'm rooting for you two," he said. "I love how happy she makes you, and as a friend, I will do whatever I can to help you two make things work."

"And how will you help us all the way from Ottawa?"

"Well," he said, "I can always help you two when you both move to Ottawa."

"Do you think Seth will too?"

He shrugged. "He's talked about it before. He might. That'd be cool. Having the four of us all together up there." He smiled and nodded. "Yeah, I think I would like that."

"We all would."

Taron rested a hand on my shoulder. "We all would."

The cabin seemed dark when we made it there. We

stopped at the foot of the small stairs leading to the door. It was almost like nobody had come back from the fire. But then again, maybe they had all gone to sleep. I wouldn't have blamed them for that. It was late. I was tired. I'm sure Taron was too.

"After you," he said, opening up the door. The common area was dimly lit, which was odd. Somebody had broken out the foam tiles and stuck them together in a crude fort in the middle of the room. Kinda strange. Nobody had used those tiles since the start of the camp, at least that I had seen.

Walking by them was the mistake I made. When I got close enough, a person erupted out of the little fort and scared the shit out of me. I nearly leapt into Taron's arms, but he nearly leapt into mine. Within seconds, Seth's and Jasmine's laughter erupted into the silence of the room and the lights clicked on.

The four of us all laughed for a minute or two. And that's the moment I realized that, like Taron, this is what I would want as well. I wanted the four of us to keep making stupid little happy moments like this one. I could live in this moment, just soak up the feeling and let it drown me.

TWENTY-SEVEN

Jasmine rested her head in my lap as Taron came back into the common room with four hot chocolates on a little tray. He sat down and handed them to each of us. I took Jasmine's for her so she wouldn't have to move yet. It's like when a pet lies down on you and gets comfy. It's law that you can't move until they do.

"Thanks," Seth said, taking a small sip. "Shame there can't be some rum in this."

"Shame," I agreed.

Jasmine blew a raspberry at me to get my attention. "Wanna take a walk?"

"At this time?" I asked her, turning to see the clock on the wall reading past midnight.

She nodded. "We can take our hot chocolates and go look at some stars."

I helped Jasmine stand up and got up with her. "We'll be back, boys. Don't stay up too late."

"You either," Seth said as Jasmine took my hand and we walked towards the door to go outside. The night was cooler now than before. And quieter. All the campers and counsellors retreated back into their dorms or just inside. The nighttime was again how it was supposed to be; just Jasmine and I.

Jasmine took a sip of hot chocolate. "This is nice."

"The hot chocolate or the night?"

She shrugged. "Both, I guess. Did you have fun at the campfire?"

"I did, yeah." I smiled and took her free hand in mine as I took a sip of the hot chocolate. I guess in the dark we had to walk a little slower so we didn't spill the hot drinks all over each other. I silently thanked her for not pushing us to walk any faster, because I for sure would have wiped out and spilled the drink on her. "So what spurred the walk?"

She shrugged again. "It's kind of our thing. We go for walks. We go for pseudo-adventures." She smiled at me. "You do like taking walks, right?"

I nodded. "With you? Of course I do."

"It's good for exercise too." She sipped her drink softly. "And I was thinking we could sneak out for the *whole* night tonight."

"Oh? Up to no good, are we?"

"If one were to look at it that way." She smirked. "I told Seth to cover for you and Shelby's covering for me. Just in case something happens. It shouldn't. And we'll be back before the counsellors wake up at ten or whenever. Our windows are unlocked. I'm smart, you see, so I planned ahead for this."

"You should go to school for being a project manager. You have a real talent for planning."

She scoffed at me and took another sip of her drink. "I mean, I might do that. That'd be a decent career, right? Remind me to search up how much they make in average salary and then we'll talk."

"Probably a lot."

"I'd sure hope so."

"Me too. Being the top guy on a project should get you some serious payout."

"But," she said, "in this economy, it probably doesn't."

I took a long sip of my hot chocolate. "You haven't told me where we're going."

"Well, that's cuz we're just going for a little walk. Maybe we don't *have* to be going anywhere." She smiled at me. "But we're going back over to the beach."

"For another campfire?"

"Do you want to have another campfire?"

Shrugging, I replied, "Maybe I do. But I can't just tell you."

"So we'll have a small little fire." She squeezed my hand. "Roast some more marshmallows maybe. Fuck, I'd even set up a fondue. Dee have a fondue?"

"I'd have a fondue."

"I wish we had a fondue."

I wished that too. Fondue late at night with Jasmine would be truly wonderful. That would have been a magical evening in the making. "Maybe we can just go steal a pot and some chocolate and have a broke fondue over the bonfire?"

Jasmine laughed. "Sounds like way too much work to me."

"Give me the keys and I'll go get everything for us."

She laughed again and shook her head. "We can do it another night. Tonight, I just wanna relax with you. Have a quiet night. No shenanigans. Just us."

"Just the two of us," I said in a singsong.

Jasmine smiled widely. "You're so cute." She tugged my arm down a small path. "This way. We're taking the scenic route."

"Okay," I muttered. I took a sip of hot chocolate and walked with her down the path. We didn't talk much. We just enjoyed each other's silent company and enjoyed the dark, spooky forest and all the weird noises coming from it. She held my hand a little tighter as we walked. Maybe she was a little scared. Maybe she thought I was. I didn't ask either way.

"We're here," she said as we arrived at the Writer's Shed (name depending on who you ask, I suppose).

"Oh, we were coming to the shed!" I set down my drink to open the door for us. "Why didn't you just say so?"

"Because it was a surprise." Jasmine smiled. "I thought it would be nice for us to sneak away and have a night together."

I smiled and nodded as I picked up my drink. "I think it's a great idea." I moved inside the shed and fumbled around for the small lamp. Once I found it, I turned it on and the shed lit up in a soft, warm light.

"So now what?" Jasmine asked as she jumped onto the bed to sit down.

I shut the door and turned the lock (for safety) and sat down next to her. "I don't know. This was *your* idea. What do you wanna do?"

"Cuddle," she said with a mischievous smile.

"I can do that." We got closer together and she rested her head on my shoulder, sipping sideways out of her hot chocolate. She was careful not to spill any on us. I took a sip of mine and we sat there and finished our drinks.

"This is nice." She grabbed the cup from me and set it down on the nearby table and she wrapped her arms around me. "I wish we could stay here forever."

"I wish we could too." I gave her a soft kiss on the forehead which warranted a wide smile to stretch across her face.

She sat upright and looked me over. "We could stay here. Live off the land. Never go back."

"We don't know the first thing about survival."

She pouted. "Yeah, no kidding. Humanity has become so dependent on being civilized." She rested her head back down on me. "But a girl can dream."

"Maybe we can go home and do some research and then meet each other in the woods."

"Yeah, that's a good idea. We can watch a bunch of survival TV shows and practise our mud hut skills in our backyards."

I chuckled. "Can't help but feel like my parents would not want me to have a singular mud hut in the backyard, let alone several with varying degrees of competency."

"I think mine would be okay with it. Probably would support it. The only time I really leave the house is when I'm here at camp. Part of why they made me go in the first place."

"What, like you wouldn't be here on your own accord anyway."

"Maybe. I guess we'll never know unless we can build a machine to take us to another dimension."

I smiled. "Yes. One where we *do* know how to survive in the wild perhaps?"

"Would we have to kill the versions of us in that universe, or do you think we would become those versions automatically and take their place?"

Shrugging, I laid back on the bed. "I think there'd be two versions of each of us."

"You mean I get two boyfriends?" Jasmine asked with a wry smile. "We could go on double dates."

"I think we're not allowed to talk to other versions of us. That's one of the first rules of time travel or interdimensional travel."

"Rules are meant to be broken," she stated.

I shrugged. "I have to disagree. I think these rules are pretty serious."

I felt Jasmine shuffling around a little, trying to get comfortable I'd assume. When I looked over, she was reaching for a blanket that she was still mostly sitting on top of. She sighed and got up to pull the blanket free. She turned off the lamp, shrouding us in relative darkness. She sat back down and laid herself next to me, covering the two of us with the blanket. "There. Now we're nice and cozy."

"I do enjoy being cozy with you."

She rested her head on my chest and looked up to you. "And I with you."

"Are you gonna go to sleep?"

"I'm not tired yet."

I smiled and kissed her forehead. "Me either."

Jasmine perked up and kissed me. I could feel her softly smiling as she did. We kissed for a few minutes and then she pulled away and just stared at me. Her eyes reflecting the soft moonlight coming in from the nearby window.

"You're beautiful," I told her.

She smiled wider. "This is one of the most clichéd moments of my life."

"As someone who loves clichés, I see no problems with it."

"Me either." Jasmine climbed on top of me and looked down on me. Her hair fell around her face, framing her mischievous smile. "So I've been thinking."

"Are you ever not?"

She slapped my shoulder lightly. "I meant about us. About how perfect this summer has been because of you."

"And?"

"And how we're running out of summer at an alarmingly quick rate."

I took a deep breath. "And?"

"And that I want to be yours, in some part, forever. That this summer is the best summer of my life, probably will be forever. From here on out, every summer will be shadowed by stress and school and work and a whole number of dumb things. But *this* summer is shadowed by you. And I like this shade."

"You are such a dork. Perhaps the biggest one in the world."

Her eyes rolled and she couldn't hold back the smile. "I

just don't want to miss out on as many good memories as I can make with you."

"We leave for home in a few days. How much more can we squeeze in?"

She shrugged. "I'm sure we can think of something." Her hand traced my collarbones. "To squeeze in."

At first, I cocked my eyebrow and gave her a weird look. But then I knew what she meant. Sex. Of course. I smiled at her and pulled her down into me. Our lips met and it felt like we had crashed into each other. She had made up her mind that this was what she wanted. She was fearless with it too. I could admire that. She knew what she wanted.

I could think of every cliché in the book to describe how it felt like our two souls were melting together as one. The way her skin felt on mine. The way her messy hair tangled in my fingers. The way her eyes wanted nothing more than for more of me to look at. Her busy hands working around me. Her busy mouth kissing me. The way the world fizzled out like the orange sodas we had been drinking all summer long.

She put the cap on the summer. Something she thought was a deserving fit, though clichéd as it was, to a summer romance gone by. And that in a few days when we leave for home, she thought it would be enough to tide us over until the next time we saw each other.

If we ever saw each other again.

THE FALL

TWENTY-EIGHT

*

Dee was fast asleep next to me in the shed. I lied next to him still naked, wrapped in the blanket and one of his arms. I kissed his cheek and crawled slowly over him. I had to slink bank to an outhouse to go pee. I got my clothes back on as quietly as I could and then snuck out the door of the shed into the night.

My legs were still shaking from the nervousness. I don't think I really planned on having sex with him tonight. But it was really now or never. I didn't regret it. I kind of just wished we had done it earlier so we could have done it more. Not like he would have been complaining about that.

Once was not enough to get me through the next few months until I would get a chance to see Dee again. If I even get to see him again. I was still so terrified of him going home and forgetting about me when he gets caught back up in life with friends and school. I was so worried that I would be left to rot in my room.

I guess I had Fred. My sweet cabbage, after all, would keep me company. Or my stuffed otter I kept at home. Unoriginally, I named him Otter. Couldn't figure out a suiting name for him. But those are my friends. Shelby doesn't go to my school, so she doesn't count the same.

I sighed and headed back towards an outhouse. Caught up in thinking, I tripped over a small rock. I picked it up and threw it into the lake. As far as I could. I watched the water ripple from the splash of the rock and then headed to pee.

I made it back to the shed and locked the door behind me. I was worried I'd have gotten caught out there and then Dee would have woken up alone and I would have felt terrible if that had happened. But I was back safe. I locked the door, undressed again, and crawled back into his warm embrace. Thank God he was a heavy sleeper.

The day we had to go home had arrived so much sooner than I was ready for. Watching Dee lug his bags to his family's car was heartbreaking. It was the final sentence in our story. We both loaded our cars and then met by the shed to say goodbye one last time. We made sure we had added each other on every conceivable thing. And swapped numbers and all that. We kissed and had we not wasted so much time sad about missing each other, we could have snuck in a quickie.

Dee kissed my forehead and smiled at me. "We'll still chill in the fall?"

I nodded. "Of course. We'll find a way to see each other. We'll make this work. It's only a short time, and then we can be together again and it'll be perfect." I knew we were both unsure of the distance. Being young is stupid though. It's like everything has to be rushed. We're always so worried about running out of time even though we have so much.

He smiled. He liked that idea. "Make sure Fred is well fed."

"Fred's gonna feed me." I rubbed my stomach. "Could go for some coleslaw right about now."

Dee just shook his head and we walked back to the cars. I watched him get into his and then the car drove away. I've never had a single tear fall from eye. It's either none or many. But one tear ran down my cheek. I don't know how I wasn't sobbing on the floor. It was painful to watch that one happy memory drive down the dusty little road.

I turned and got into my car. Earbuds in. Music up. I texted Dee the whole way home. He was just as sad as I was to see me out of the rear window, standing there in the gravel with a sad face on.

I tried to do my best to not think about it in the following few days, but it was hard not to. He was all I could think about for weeks at a time. I had gotten home and tried to unpack, but I would smell him on my clothes and get sad. I would look at the notebook of poems and writing and see his notes and poems he wrote in my notebook and drawings and doodles and the summer would keep rushing back into my head.

The memories were vibrant and orange and warm. When I tried to have an orange soda, I thought about him. When I saw my body in the mirror, I traced the places he touched me, the places he kissed me. I watched my body in the mirror, living through the memory of that night. I couldn't even shower without thinking about him.

Weeks ticked by. School came at us in full force. I noticed he texted less during school and it only reinforced my fears and anxieties about being forgotten and left behind. We tried to make plans within the first week we were at school, but they fell apart because, well, we lived too far apart and neither of us can drive and our parents are pretty busy and generally didn't care about our summer fling.

But in the fall, when the trees began to turn orange and

red and yellow and cover the ground in their palette, we made progress. We agreed to just say fuck it and ride our bikes to each other for a day trip.

We had a phone call one night where he had a breakdown about his life. It ended with him telling me how grateful he was to have met me and have gone to the camp, despite how stupid camps were in his opinion. I was just as grateful for him showing up. He kept contact with Seth and Taron as well. So it gave me more hope that we could work this out.

It was after this little breakdown that we made the bike plans. To meet up the weekend after Thanksgiving at a halfway point between the two of us at a café or something similar to hang out and kiss. I would have loved it more if we could book a hotel room and have a night together.

But we're too young.

And we're in love.

And those two things,

Seldom mix well.

TWENTY-NINE

Today was the day! I finally get to see Dee. It had been seven or eight weeks since I had seen him last, and quite frankly, Skype calls just aren't the same as seeing him in the flesh. I can't kiss him through a screen. We set out to meet each other near a little ice cream shop on a warm autumn day. It was roughly smack dab in between us. In a little town near the lake. Perfect for a cute day with my Dee.

I made sure to wear something cute. A sundress and long socks. Cute shoes. I had my mom do my hair up in a French braid. We had a conversation where he mentioned he liked that look. So I figured I would bust it out for today, though it wasn't very comfortable in a helmet, which I had to wear because I wasn't gonna get away with riding that far without some safety measures.

The ride wasn't intolerably long, but it was long enough that my poor legs were sore from pedalling. I made it to the ice cream shop first. I had brought my notebook (just in case).

I sat and wrote some poems and did some doodling for twenty minutes until I heard the unmistakable sound of a bike rolling up. Dee hopped off and dropped the bike to the dirt.

I jolted towards him and we hugged. Then kissed. And hugged more. He lifted me up and swung me around and around, kissing me all over.

"I missed you!" he said as he put me down.

"Not nearly as much as I missed you." I smiled at him and he sat down next to me.

He picked up the notebook and leafed through it. "You were writing, huh?"

"I was *waiting*." I nudged him a little. "But yeah, I was working on some stuff."

"Poems?"

"Yeah. Duh."

"Come on, let's get some ice cream." He smirked. "That's the real reason I came all the way out here." So we got up and went to get the ice cream. He looked different than before. More toned in a way. Like he lost weight in the last two months.

"Have you thought about your college yet?"

"I'm gonna take a writing program. I might as well chase a career in the only thing I'm good at." He laughed a little and started working on his ice cream cone.

I went to lick my cone, but the ice cream tipped over the side and fell onto the ground. It was hot enough that the ice cream began melting pretty quickly. We both laughed a little. It was only ice cream, who cares. "That's me when I first met you. Melted. Little puddle."

"You're so cute," he said with a smile. He shared his ice cream with me as we sat down on the nearby bench and caught up. It was nice to be able to hold his hand and rest my head on his shoulder and to kiss him. Being away from him really made me want him all that much more, not less. He was smiling from ear to ear and so happy to see me as well.

"I don't want us to ever have to leave," I grumbled.

He rested his hand on my thigh. "I know." His face grows sombre, seemingly out of nowhere. Like clouds rolling in on a sunny day, the entire atmosphere changed. This wasn't a happy face. This wasn't a face I ever wanted to see on him.

"Are you okay?"

"I've just been thinking. About us."

My heart beat heavy in my throat. *Fuck.* "What about us?"

"I don't think we should be worried about each other right now." He looked at me with a reserved and sombre expression. Followed by what equates to a slammed-door statement. "I think we should break up."

I bit my lip and nodded. "That's... what you want?"

"I think so." He hung his head. "I just think we bonded our hearts too tight. It was like we suffocated them. And that's not our fault. But we let our hopes get too high and it's not fair for us to spend the next entire year, the most important one in our young lfe, pent up and worried about this. I don't want us to ruin our futures for each other. Because, let's face it, people make stupid decisions for love. If we're both in Ottawa in a year or two, then we can do this again. Properly."

I had to fight back tears now. "I understand." But the thing about me is that I'm a terrible fighter. Within seconds, I had streaks of tears down my cheeks. "You came all this way to break up with me?"

"I came all this way to see you."

"To break up with me."

He frowned softly and turned away. "In a way. But I just needed to see you."

"You could have just told me at camp and I would have understood."

"I thought I could do this."

"I thought you could too."

He squeezed my thigh. "You're special, Jasmine. And I'm sorry. And I wish I didn't have to do this to feel okay, but I'm a ball of stress and anxiety since I've been back at school. I need to focus on myself. I don't know what else to do."

I stood up and took a deep breath. "Okay."

"I don't want you to be mad at me."

"I'm not mad, you idiot. I'm fucking upset."

He stood up and hugged me. "I'm sorry. Please let me know when you get home safe." He turned and picked up his bike. Our whole day lasted 147 minutes. Enough time to catch up, to eat some ice cream, and then to break up with me.

I picked up my bike and fastened my helmet on as I watched him ride away. This time, not just one tear, but many, too many to ever count, so many that I couldn't see. I wished my eyes had wipers or something.

I wished I could erase my feelings. I wished that it would stop. That this was a dream I could wake up from. But I rode home. All the way. My legs burning by the time I reached my driveway from how hard I was pedalling. I was upset and angry at the situation.

I was scared of being alone and now here I was, all alone again. And I was scared of losing the person who understood me best in the whole world. And here I was, without the very person that made me feel like I would be okay.

The best summer of my life quickly flipped into the worst autumn of my life. And the longest winter. The spring, of course, would be overwhelmingly stressful while trying to get ready for college and figuring out that mess.

The year, as shit as it was, would have been bearable with Dee waiting at the end of the rainbow for me. I had something to work for. Us. And now that's gone.

I texted him that I got home safe and then deleted his number. Erased him from my life. I couldn't bear to see his face on social media. I didn't need to subject myself to that every time I tried to catch up on memes or my other friends, the few I did have.

Seemingly, just as quickly as he arrived into my life, he

was departed again. He didn't try to talk to me much after that. Mostly a few texts asking how I was. By the end of the calendar year, he had stopped altogether. Probably because I would only give him one-world replies and never do my part in carrying a conversation. I didn't want to. I couldn't bring myself to talk to him without crying or telling him I missed him and that I wanted to try again.

He understood that. Of course he did. He's a smart guy after all. That's part of why I liked hm. Smart and caring and funny. He was really the whole package for me.

I couldn't mope about him all year though. Like I mentioned, college was approaching fast. I had made my choice of program (a generic business program). I made arrangements to room with some girls from a poetry club at the school who I became okay friends with and they happened to be going to the same school. Oddly, one of them was taking a professional writing course. And I silently prayed she would never end up talking to Dee if they were in shared classes.

I made plans to move and to move on. I didn't see or hear from Dee in my first year of college, despite that I knew he was also going to the same school. I did talk to Seth and Taron occasionally and they only ever told me that he was doing okay, which is likely the same thing they told him if he ever asked about me.

Which I doubt he did.

But I could hope.

But I think him thinking and asking about me would cough up all my old emotions and that just wouldn't be very good for me. Not while I'm trying to get through my schooling. Not for him either. He's probably moved on. Found a girl. Forgotten about me. Just like I always knew he would. Because that's my role in these stories. I'm the forgettable one.

TWO YEARS LATER

THIRTY

Before my second year, my roommates both ended up dating someone. Which left me as a token loner, sitting at home doing homework and being, well, lonely. Just like how I had spent my high school years. All that FOMO came crashing back in pretty quickly. Especially since neither of them told me all that much about their boyfriends. I felt way outside the loop.

"Delilah," I said, glaring at her. "Tell me about him. How'd you guys meet?"

She rolled her eyes. "He's in my class. He's a writer."

I chewed the inside of my lip. "How long have you been seeing him then?"

She sighed and rolled her head back. "Maybe a month or so. We've been fooling around since before then." Delilah was a nerd though. So this was a big deal for her to be with someone. She had big glasses and tons of freckles. A classic redhead look, if we're being honest. But her hair was always up in some 1980s curls. Little too dated if you asked me. But it worked on her.

"And Madison. I feel like you're never home anymore." Delilah and I turned to Madison. A stupidly smart girl. She was shorter than Delilah, around my height, and also worse big glasses. What set her apart from us distinctly, was our food choices. Delilah and I were very white with our food, and Madison, being Puerto Rican and having family in Louisiana, loved a much wider variety of foods. Which was nice when she cooked, because then Delilah and I were exposed to something other than chicken and veggies.

"I work 44 hours a week and have school 47 weeks a year. All my free time gets devoted to my boyfriend. I'm sorry that I'm not around much," she said, sipping out of her beer. "I wish I could be though because you girls are my girls and I love you."

"When do we get to meet your boyfriend?" Delilah asked her.

Madison laughed softly. "When do we get to meet yours?"

"You can guys can meet mine," I said, holding up a small bottle of John Swigwell (a brand of rum that I frequented). The girls and I shared a good laugh over that one. My loneliness has not made me bitter. I refused that notion.

"That's a snack," Delilah noted.

I reclined back in my seat and took a sip of my drink. "I never really thought about being the kind of person that just sits here and drinks for *fun*."

"Writers are more likely to become alcoholics," Madison noted. "That's a science fact right there."

"That's a sad fact," Delilah said. She took a sip of her drink. "Are we all alcoholics?"

"High-functioning alcoholics if we are," I told her. "I like to think we're towing the line well enough to avoid that distinction though."

"Well, back to the boyfriend thing. We should plan a little

thing for some time soon. It'd be nice for our boys to meet the girls," Madison suggested. "My boyfriend is usually too busy with shit to focus on having a social life half the time. He has, like, two friends."

"So do we," Delilah said as she finished off her drink. She got up to pour herself another one. "But yeah, all my boyfriend does is lock himself away and write or play games and then it's work and school. I can barely convince him to give me attention sometimes."

"The struggle," I teased. I handed her my glass and got her to top up my drink. It was planned to be a long night of drinking. We were celebrating a successful summer of doing pretty much nothing but work and writing. I really enjoyed living with two other poets. We all just *got* each other. So it was a very nice atmosphere to be in.

"My boyfriend is free tomorrow night," Madison told us, setting her phone down. "Delilah, your move."

"I'll ask him, but no promises."

"I'll go shopping for some snacks and stuff," I said. "I don't mind being a generous host for them. I'm excited to *finally* meet them."

"You should find a date too," Madison suggested, staring at me with a look of intent.

I laughed it off. "No way."

"What about that cute guy in your accounting class?"

"I know of no such guy."

"Yeah, yeah." Delilah took a sip. "What was his name again? Bart?"

I mimed making myself throw up. "More like barf."

"So you're just gonna hang out and be the fifth wheel?" Delilah asked.

I nodded. "Of course. I don't mind being the fifth wheel. I wanna meet these boys that are stealing away my girls."

Madison smirked and Delilah nodded her head. And we just drank and laughed the night away. I wondered a lot about Delilah's boyfriend. A lot of what she said about him sounded like things that could be said about Dee as well. I wonder why neither him nor I have talked to each other. We haven't even *seen* each other since that fateful autumn day when we called it quits.

But he was right. We were young. We let our hopes get too high. Or maybe I just let my anxieties get the better of me and ruin everything. Something like a self-fulfilling prophecy. Maybe. That's probably the most likely thing that happened. It's so often times that humans will obsess about a thought and saying out loud that bad things will happen, and subconsciously, we drive ourselves to that same outcome. Maybe we should externalize positive outcomes a little more often. Maybe then we'd be getting somewhere.

The next day, I woke up (as one normally does, I suppose). And it was my solemn duty to gather snacks for the night ahead. I heard the familiar pitter-pattering of rain on my bedroom window. I feel like it's always raining in this city. At least in the past few weeks it's been raining a lot. It makes me feel glum and down in the dumps. And I'm already lonely and sad, so adding rain to my melancholic life didn't help. Not even a little. Not even Fred or orange soda made me feel the same. (Yes, I kept a cabbage in my fridge named Fred still.)

On my way to the store, I decided to walk and risk getting a cold from being in the rain. The rain came down hard and fast, and the wind was bitter and cold. How was it so damn cold in the middle of late summer? I thought back on all my past summers and how I couldn't remember a day where it was under fifteen and rainy before October even. Or maybe I have shit memory.

I gathered all my snacks. I got us chips, and pops, and chocolates, and charcuterie. As a nineteen-year-old girl, I was over the moon about charcuterie. That's the new "it" thing.

If you don't like charcuterie, I don't like you. It's been decided. It's still fuck pineapple on pizza too, while we're at it.

Once back in the warmth of the apartment, I drop my bag of goods onto the counter and find my little backpack with my notebook and laptop in it. I head back out into the winds and rains. I still had some time to kill before the girls and their boys came over. So I headed down to my favourite little café to do some work on writing and perhaps my next poetry collection.

Because, as I haven't mentioned it, I self-published my first poetry collection! All by my lonesome. I know. I'm just as proud. It sold well enough in the first few weeks. I felt so accomplished and happy about it being done, let alone other people *actually* liking it. And then I always wondered, too, if Dee ever bought it or ever even saw it online. I took out his submissions. It felt wrong to include them since we weren't really talking anymore. I know he wanted me to put them in there, but I just couldn't.

"French vanilla, no whip, with a shot of espresso, please and thank you" I told the barista, who nodded and turned to start my order.

"French vanilla," a voice said from behind me in line. "I guess orange sodas aren't much of a rainy-day drink, huh?"

My head swivelled around and my eyes shot wide. The voice belonged to a familiar enough face. One I hadn't seen since that fateful day in autumn. The voice belonged to a person that looked much older, taller, and defined. "Dee?"

THIRTY-ONE

My fingers wrapped around the warm cup of French vanilla as Dee sits in front of me with his Americano. It seems our drink choices matured just a little bit. Maybe as much as we did. Or maybe, like our exteriors, it was a cover for a lack of maturity.

"I can't believe it took this long to bump into each other," Dee said, sipping a small bit of his coffee. "I've been around this area all summer too."

"What for?"

"My girlfriend lives around here," he told me. "So I end up dropping her off and walking around with her around here. Some of my friends are around here too. I was actually coming back from an all-nighter at my friend's."

"An all-nighter? Are we still in high school?" I laughed softly, trying to make sure he knew it was a joke.

He laughed softly too. "I guess we never really leave high school, huh?"

"Nope. Just like that classic rock song always said."

He smiled. I missed his smile. I never knew I could miss a smile so much. "How have you been?"

"Um." My brain stalled on me. *Fuck, say something.* "I've been okay."

"Okay? Just okay?" He scoffed. "The past two years have been a rollercoaster and we haven't spoken to each other in over a year. I have zero idea what your life has been like." He took a long sip of his coffee. "Do you have a boyfriend?"

I shook my head. "Hard no."

"Did you finish your poetry collection?"

I nodded. "I suppose, though, finished is a sort of subjective term. I never think anything is finished, but when it starts to creep into those really high page counts, I had to trim it down and cut it off."

"And?" His eyes were wide. "Did you publish it?"

I nodded again, smiling a little. I can't help but be proud of myself. Even self-publishing can be tricky. "I self-published it. You can buy it on most online marketplaces and e-book stores."

He smiled wide. "Jasmine! I'm so proud of you!"

"Stop, you're making me blush!"

"How many copies have you sold?"

I shrugged. "Maybe a couple hundred over the time it's been up."

"And you're working on a follow-up, I assume?"

I nodded. "Of course. What about your book?"

Rolling his eyes, he sighed loudly. "What about my book?"

"Did you do anything with it? Is it finished?"

"I mean, yeah. It's done. But I haven't done anything with it, nor do I even know how to. I just have a manuscript taking up space in my computer now. I've starting working on other stuff too. More poems and stuff. Another two novels." He took another sip and looked at me quizzically. "Did you ever add those poems I gave you?"

I laughed softly. "No. I know you told me too, but I couldn't bring myself to put things you wrote into my collection when we had stopped talking. Maybe the next one though." I winked at him as I took another sip of coffee. "If I ever get around to a next one."

"You will." He smiled and took my hand. "It's in your blood to write, and so write you will."

"How's your girlfriend?" I asked, pulling my hand away. I didn't want us to develop the wrong idea of this rekindling.

He cleared his throat. "She's okay. Works a lot. Too busy for me most of the time, so I end up sitting around sad and alone most nights, but I guess the time we do spend together is pretty nice." He looked off out the window to the empty distant sky. "She's *okay* though."

"That doesn't like she's *okay*." We both paused and I think we both spaced out for a moment. I snapped myself back into focus. "Wait, so you don't also work a lot? I'm either in class or at work, I feel like. I'm always tired and up late."

"I mean, my job pays me a little nicer than hers so she works more, and my hours fit easier into my schedule and my job is closer than hers. So I just get more time off." He sighed and looked intently at his coffee cup. "I'm not entirely sure she's even working all the time. I'm probably just too much for her sometimes, I think. She says I'm emotionally distant at times. Maybe I'm worrying for nothing and she *is* always working, but I mean, I think the emotional distance is a factor. Wouldn't you?"

"Like, she's working or lying about working to get out of having to deal with your emotional distance?"

Dee sighed again. "That sounds even stupider when you say it. Fuck."

"Dee, as soon as people start worrying about shit, their minds get all irrational and fucked up. Like with us. I thought my anxiety pulled *us* apart."

"But it was mine," Dee stated. "I know."

"I was gonna say it was just poor timing and lack of experience on our ends," I said, taking his hand back in mine, "because it wasn't really either of us."

"But it was. I mean, I cut it off. We probably would have made it if not for that."

"I don't think we would have."

"No?"

"No. Looking back, I think it was the right choice."

Dee frowned. "I don't."

"I know. But we have a chance to be friends again. Without any resentment. This *is* what we wanted in the end."

"Is it what you wanted?" he asked. His eyes scanned my face for any sign of emotion. I couldn't just tell him something he wanted to hear without lying to one of us. I did want us to be friends in the end, because he ended the chance of us being something more, but I wanted us to be something more though, even if he didn't. He wanted me to say no. But I wanted to say yes.

"I don't know what I wanted," I told him instead. "I only know what I didn't want."

"Which was what?"

"Losing you completely," I said. "I never wanted you to be gone forever."

"I never wanted to go forever."

I squeezed his hand a little. "So why did you stop replying to me out of nowhere?"

"I got jealous."

"Of what?"

"Of that stupid guy you used to talk about," Dee said, rolling his eyes a bit. "I know it's dumb, but so was I. I was an insecure teenager. Still am, I guess, technically."

"That guy was just a friend. He ended up dating another one of my friends anyway, which you would have known I was setting them up if you let me explain the situation."

"I'm sorry for how I acted, Jasmine."

"Me too, Dee. Moving forward, however," I said with a

deep breath. "We should try this whole friends thing again. I think I'd like that."

He smiled. "I'd like that too."

"Good. That being said, my roommates are bringing their boyfriends over tonight, and I don't wanna ride stag to this thing, so will you be my plus one? As a friend?"

He laughed softly. "Sure. I can't stay long. My girlfriend also invited me over to a thing tonight. She never invites me to events or gatherings, so I assume it's pretty important."

"I'll text you my address?"

*

Jasmine stood up from the table and gave me one last smile after having written her number down on the napkin. I sat there looking at it. It was the same number as before. I never deleted her number from my phone, but I guess this means she had deleted mine. I don't blame her I suppose. We had fallen out of touch after we broke up and in the few weeks and months after that, my trust issues crept up and damaged what little relationship we had left. Just like that, the summer romance had been replaced with a fall breakup and winter fights. Fizzled out like flat soda.

I finished my drink and went home to shower and change and get ready for a long night. Jasmine's little gathering and then my girlfriend's afterwards. I would surely be up late tonight. Probably not for good reasons. I'm never up late for good reasons.

I guess good reasons would be different for most people. Sex, drinking, friends, parties, a good dinner, writing, painting, watching TV or movies.

But I'm up late because of anxiety, fights with the girlfriend, stressing over school. The list goes on. It started around when Jasmine and I dropped contact. Something about her just calmed me down, even though I acted like a total jackass towards the end.

So, when she left my life, I spent two years or thereabouts in a spiral. I've been sad and melancholic and, for lack of a better term, I've been fucked up. I started dating a girl here that doesn't haven't time for me, but it's better to have somebody distant (like I have been to her lately) than to not have anybody. Loneliness has become the biggest taboo in the modern era, I think. Nobody wants to be alone. Nobody wants to *admit* that they're alone, or that they feel alone. Not in this world of dating apps and social media. Being lonely is, apparently, the worst thing a person can be.

And that's why I stay with someone that doesn't make me happy. Because the comfort of having someone, *anyone,* is better than being lonely.

After my shower, I fix my hair and find something nice to wear. I had been texting Jasmine about her address and what I should wear, bring, and what to expect. Her apartment isn't that far away from me in all actuality, so I decided I would just take the thirty-minute walk to get some of my nerves out on the way. I hadn't seen her in so long. The coffee talk got my heart racing quick enough as it were.

I went out into the day again and started walking. I put on my favourite few songs and that was enough for me. Something about music and walking just goes hand in hand for me.

Once I arrived at Jasmine's, she came down to meet me in the lobby of her building. It wasn't terribly tall, but tall enough. I think she mentioned she lived on the seventh floor. I wish I lived on the seventh floor, beats a basement apartment's view by a mile. Plus, the breeze coming in through the window would be way better up higher.

"Long time, no see," Jasmine said as she beams at me from the lobby. She had slipped on large wool slippers with floppy ears to come down. I honestly expected that out of her too. She looked so much older. The past two years had been kind to her. Her softness was replaced with a slender grace. Her cheeks slimmed and her jawbones stuck out a little further than I remembered before. Her legs were more toned. Her hair was longer, and wavier than it had been before. I wonder if she thought the same things of me. Or if I just look the exact same as I always did. I feel like I didn't change at all, or at the very least, I didn't change very much.

"I know. It's been at least a few hours."

"It's been a year if it's been an hour," she said with a small smile. "Would you like to come up and say hi to everyone?"

"There's an everyone?" I asked.

She smiled and nodded. "All four of them, yeah. Not a very big everyone."

"Big enough. Bigger than what I usually have to deal with."

"Are you nervous?" she asked as she called the elevator. Side note: I always love how elevator buttons light up around them after you press them. I dunno, I guess I just think it's a cool aesthetic.

I shrugged. "Maybe I am a little nervous. Meeting new people is stressful."

"I bet it is for you." She grabbed my arm and led me into the elevator. "I think you'll be fine. You handled the camp well."

"The camp was less intimate."

"For some," she said. The elevator fell silent. I think we both started thinking about each other was all. That first night we spent together. It was special. It was perfect. It was a number of other adjectives I'm too lazy to think of. I wondered how often she had thought of that night. I wondered if she had any other nights just like it. "Sorry." Her voice felt so small. She hadn't stepped over a line or anything, but maybe she thought she did.

I reached my hand down towards hers and smiled at her. "It's okay. We're okay. You're okay." I gave her hand a small squeeze.

"Okay. No more awkwardness."

"Okay. Agreed."

She smiled at me and the elevator dinged as the door opened up. She led me out into a rather rustic-looking hallway. The kind with old brown walls and musty carpets with that weird design I had previously thought was only reserved for the couches at a grandmother's house.

I followed her into the apartment and instantly, all I could smell was her perfume. I could tell she lived here. The whole place hit me like a wave of memories. The same smells from two years ago, back at the campgrounds when we would sit too close together at assemblies or in class or on the beach.

"You okay?" Jasmine asked me.

I nodded and let myself get introduced to everybody. But you don't care about everybody. Because this story isn't about everybody. It's about me and Jasmine (and to some extent about Seth and Taron, but they're not here right now). So I'll save the trouble of writing all the small talk and skip ahead to the more important stuff.

THRTY-TWO

Everybody had left Jasmine's apartment and left the two of us alone. She had ordered a pizza, no pineapples of course. I wasn't hungry enough to eat much of it, so there we sat with a half-eaten pizza collecting dust on the coffee table. She rested her feet on my legs and we scrolled our phones out of the awkwardness of being alone together like this again. I mean, small talk would flare up once in a while, but we probably spent a solid hour sitting like that on the couch.

She kicked my stomach lightly. "Wanna do something?"

I cocked an eyebrow. "Like what?"

"Like… an adventure?"

"Like… what kind of adventure are we talking about here?"

"Like, an adventure-y kind." She smiled softly. "I never thought you'd be one to ask too many questions. Usually you just say yes and go along with me."

"I still will. I'm just curious."

She swung her legs over and sat upright. "Okay. So I'll let you know when I know. But for now, let's roll out." She stood up and picked up a knitted sweater and put it on. The sleeves were too long for her, so she rolled them up and smiled at me. "I actually think I want a snack. There's a market nearby here that has amazing deep-fried cheesecake balls."

"Deep-fried cheesecake balls?" I stood up and nodded. "You should have lead with that. Let's get going. You're getting me all hungry."

The walk to the market was very long, but for the fifteen minutes it took, Jasmine gushed about the market and the cheesecake balls. She said they were melt-in-your-mouth gooey. I had never them so I couldn't relate to that feeling just yet.

"Come on. It's just up here." Jasmine tugged at my arm, but I wanted to stop and enjoy the sights for a moment. The dark sky above us contrasted with the bright lights of this outdoor market. The stalls were lined with bright neon lights and signs. The place was very busy for it being late evening. There were stalls all bunched together selling fish, fruits, veggies, cell phone cases, fresh doughnuts, sushi, burgers, souvenirs, playing cards, other nerdy things, and so much more. You could probably find anything in this market. It's hard to believe this was my first time here.

"This place is magnificent."

"Oh, I know, right? Innocent little farmer's market by day, playground for the bored at night."

In the distance of the market, I could see an arcade. The unmistakable shapes of arcade machines and flashing lights. Man, it really brings me back to spending days at the bowling alley with my friends growing up.

"You okay?" Jasmine asked.

I nodded. "Just observing."

"Come on! We came here for deep-fried cheesecake. The cravings are only getting stronger the closer we get." She smiled and tugged on my arm enough to dishevel my shirt. I followed her happily. I'd follow her anywhere, most likely. She made any place feel a hundred times safer. Could have been the positive vibes she exuded that helped keep me so calm around her.

The market seemed to sprawl out forever. As we walked, I couldn't help but have the thought that this place was a labyrinth. And that once you're inside of it, you can never get back out. The stalls went on and on. Lights and people and fruits and fish and the distant sounds of heating and cooling units moving stale air around. It almost felt cyberpunk in some aspects. Like I had been teleported into a rundown future version of a normal market.

Jasmine stopped us and smiled widely. "It's here. Right here, this is the place."

I eyed over the kiosk she stopped us at. There was a large line (of course) and at the kiosk was a little conveyor belt where freshly dough-coated balls of cheesecake would fall into a fryer and then the fryer would automatically flip them with a little mesh paddle and then they'd fall into a tray when done. Then they'd get covered in your choice of powder, sprinkles, or sugar.

"What flavour do you want?" Jasmine asked, looking up at the board of prices, flavours, and other offerings. They have fresh doughnuts here as well. Of course.

"There's a lot to choose from," I told her. Strawberry sugar. Vanilla sugar. Chocolate sugar. Cinnamon sugar. You can even get them drizzled with glaze and rolled in sprinkles. "I might have to try the sprinkle one. It sounds pretty extra, and I like that shit."

"I know you like that shit." She laughed softly. "I usually spend ten minutes deciding on a flavour and I always end up getting classic cinnamon sugar."

We waited in line and order our cheesecake balls. Jasmine watched me like a hawk as I tried my first bite of one.

"So! So! So! How is it?!" she asked, practically bouncing up and down.

I smiled at her and nodded my approval. "It's very good. The sprinkles were the right choice for me I think."

"I've never tried that one. Here let's swap." She handed me a cinnamon sugar one and I handed her back a sprinkled one. She popped it into her mouth and made one of the deepest groans I've ever heard her make. "Fuck, that is so good."

"They're very good." I shot her a small smile. "So what should we do next?" I put another cheesecake ball in my mouth and watched her eyes dart around are immediate area.

"Oh! I have an idea."

"What's your idea?"

"Just... follow me?" Her eyes met with mine and she gave me a soft smile. The kind of smile that would make you trust a total stranger, the kind that would make you melt where you stood, the kind that made a younger version of me fall for Jasmine in the first place.

But I followed her anyway. As we walked, I felt almost guilty. I still had a girlfriend to go home too. I shook the thought from my head. Mostly because I didn't care. But also because this was just two friends hanging out and catching up. It didn't need to be anything more than that. It *wasn't* anything more than that.

And it was that moment that my girlfriend texted me asking where I was. I had completely forgotten about the plans we had tonight up until this moment. Her message said she was at my apartment with my roommate waiting for me, but it's nearly midnight now. I had a few missed messages from her earlier too. She was not happy. I let out a groan.

"What's wrong?" Jasmine asked, turning back.

"I sort of forgot that I ditched my girlfriend tonight."

Jasmine eyes widened. "Oh, shit, I'm so sorry. Please go back and see her. I didn't mean to make you forget about your plans. I'm stupid. I'm sorry. Go."

"Jasmine, I'm already here. She's already mad. It's fine.

I'm telling her I forgot and got caught up with old friends."

"Old friends?"

"Yeah," I said, typing my message, "what's wrong with that?"

"You don't wanna tell her you're with me?" Jasmine raised an eyebrow at me.

I rolled my eyes. "She's already mad. If I tell her I'm with you, she'll probably kill me."

"Because of our history?"

"No."

Jasmine sighed. "You haven't even told her about us, have you?"

"Of course not," I replied. "She's the jealous type as is."

"Ah, I get it."

"It's not the best. I think she just wishes I were more submissive and that I would just listen to her every whim."

"That doesn't sound like a healthy relationship."

I shrugged. "How many healthy relationships do you really know?" I cocked my eyebrow. "They all have problems. Everybody's fucked up anyway."

"I guess." She chewed at her lip a little bit. "You don't think we had that many issues, do you?"

"Of course we did."

"Really?"

"You had all these anxieties about being forgotten and I was a mess that couldn't keep it together long enough to make it through the year." I put my phone back after finishing a lengthy apology text. "People aren't perfect. We all have problems. Relationships just work when your problems mesh well or if the other person knows the solutions."

"Which is rare."

"Which is rare," I repeated. "Exactly."

Jasmine tugged at my hand. "Come on. I still wanna show you this thing while we're still on our adventure."

I smiled and nodded. "Okay, let's continue."

Jasmine led me through the rest of the market, all the way to the other side. I'm surprised there was an other side with how big this place was. She stopped us in front of a metal door embedded into a grimy brick wall.

"So now we go in here," she said, opening the door.

"You're kidding me."

"Nope. Come on. After you."

I rolled my eyes. "This is sketchy as hell. I'm not going in there."

"Dee."

"Jazz."

Her voice got very stern. "Dee."

"Okay, fine." I walked past her and down the sketchy, dimly lit stairwell I found inside. I got to what looked like a lobby, though it had no markings anywhere and no posters or anything. Just a desk. At least it was a well-lit room. "What is this place?"

"Hello?" Jasmine yelled. "It's me! Jasmine!"

"Jasmine?!" a voice called back. The voice belonged to a small girl with glasses and a large purple sweater with a fish logo. She came out from out the doorway behind the desk. "Fancy seeing you here." The girl's eyes darted to me quickly. "Who's this?"

"This is Dee."

"Dee," she said. She walked over and stuck out her hand. "My name's Yasmine."

"Yasmine and Jasmine," I said with a small laugh. "Nice to meet you."

"What can I do for you tonight, Jazz?"

"Two tickets to the late-night exhibit, please."

"What, is this a museum?" I asked.

Jasmine shook her head. "No. It's way cooler."

I rolled my eyes as Yasmine handed Jasmine two tickets and Jasmine gave her a folded twenty. "So are you gonna tell me what this place is?"

"Nope. I'm gonna *show* you."

"Okay." I rolled my eyes and followed her lead through a set of double doors to our left. Yasmine went back into the back room after wishing us a fun time.

When we entered the door, my eyes had to readjust to the darkness. There were small arrow-shaped LED lights on the ground and a little strip of dim lighting along the floor where it met with the walls. There were no lights above us. Just the floor lighting, which was barely bright enough to see anything at all.

"Jasmine," I said, "what is this place?"

"Just follow my silhouette," she replied, leading the way down the dark hallway.

It was after ten more seconds when I noticed the end of the hallway was a blueish hue. Dimly lit still, but blue no doubt. As we got closer, there was a large doorway and the room inside was very tinged in blue light from a giant glass wall of water. What caught my eye was a large fish staring back at me. It was an aquarium. A massive one. Thousands of fish floating and swimming around. There were a few benches set up in front of the tank. Jasmine went over and stood in front of the tank.

"Beautiful, huh?" The light reflecting through the water began to dance on her face. I could see the whole tank reflecting in her eyes. Beautiful was an understatement.

"Yeah." I've always been mesmerized by fish and sea life and the world of the underwater. "How did you get into this place?"

"It stays open pretty late, but after it closes, which was a few minutes ago, you have to use the secret entrance." She smiled. "And I know Yasmine from school and she lets me in here while she does her end-of-day stuff. I usually come here to write."

"They don't care that you're in here all night?"

She shrugged. "They've never complained. Yasmine and the owner are pretty close and so the owner also likes me by extension."

"That's so cool." My eyes were fixed on this tank. Watching every fish just living its life, swimming around. Must be weird to be gawked at every day like this. Same concept as a zoo, you know? Weird.

I turned to Jasmine and watched her eyes looking around at the fishes. I wondered how many times she'd been in this room, and how she could still be so entranced by the tank of fish having seen it so many times. But yet here she was, staring in awe. The blue light drawing her face with a particular softness. Her sharp jawline replaced with the softer one I remembered her having from back at camp. A wave of emotions swirled inside of me.

She turned to me and smiled, turning back to the tank without saying anything about the fact that I was staring at her. In my defence, she was unconceivably more beautiful than a tank of fish.

I felt my phone going off in my pocket and I rolled my eyes. "Do you mind if I step out for a minute?" I asked Jasmine.

She nodded. "I'll be right here."

I smiled at her and went back up the dark hallway as I answered the phone.

"Where are you?!" my lovely girlfriend yelled into my ear.

"I'm at an aquarium."

"At this time of night?" She was clearly annoyed and didn't believe me. "Who are you with? Why have you been ignoring me the entire night? We had plans tonight and you disappeared."

"Samantha," I groaned. "I'm sorry. But I'm with old friends."

"Yeah, old friends you've never mentioned to me."

"Do I need to tell you every person I've ever met in my life?"

Samantha sighed. "No. Unless it's someone you *don't* want me to know about."

"Holy shit."

"So it is someone you don't want me to know about?"

"No. I don't care. You're just blowing this up. You do this every week. I'm sick of it."

"You don't usually just disappear."

"Yes, but all your texts are incessant." I wanted to just hang up and throw my phone. "You do this all the time. I don't reply to you and you send me a hundred messages and make me feel guilty for showering without telling you."

"But you're not showering now," she said. "Are you?"

"It's the principle of the thing, Sam."

She groaned and I could tell she was just mad for the sake of being mad at this point. "I want you to come home."

"I don't want to."

"Dalton."

I rolled my eyes. "I'm not coming home until *I* want to."

"Goddamn it, Dalton."

I gritted my teeth. Okay. I think it was time to just rip the bandage off on this one. I've been unhappy for so many weeks at this point anyway. "Samantha."

"What?" she barked.

"I think it's time we split up. I can't do this with you anymore. I don't want this."

She went dead silent very quickly and then let out a few whimpering attempts at a sentence. "You don't mean that. You can't."

"I think I do," I told her. I let out a small groan and start pacing at the end of the hallway. "I just can't do this anymore. Okay?"

"No, it's not okay!" she yelled.

"I'm done, Sam. I'm gonna hang up now."

She didn't say anything after that. She let me hang up the phone without a fight. Maybe because in her heart she thought the same things and felt the same way about us. I sighed and ran a hand through my hair, silently screaming in my head. I put my phone back into my pocket and walked back to where I had left Jasmine. She was still watching the all the fish swim around. Still cloaked in the soft blue light. I smiled at her.

"Girlfriend?" she asked me.

I laughed. "Not anymore."

Jasmine frowned. "Oh. I'm sorry."

"It's not your fault."

"Mmm, I feel like it is." Jasmine still frowned softly and went quiet for a few seconds. She turned to me and caught my gaze. "Can I show you something else?"

I nodded. "Of course."

THIRTY-THREE

The aquarium was a lot bigger than I thought it would have been. Jasmine walked me through a bunch of cold water aquarium exhibits, a stingray tank, a shark tank, and a local ecosystem tank. We saw shrimps, an octopus, anemones, corals, and sea urchins. I had never seen a sea urchin before until Jasmine showed me.

"It's just through here," Jasmine told me, walking up to a doorway.

"What is it?" I asked, thinking of what animals we could look at that we hadn't already. Maybe a killer whale, which would have been pretty cool. Instead of that, however, the room was cloaked in an eerie dark blue glow that changed to a dark red slowly and then back to blue. We walked onto a glass floor with glass walls surrounding us. We were basically inside the tank was how it felt. And all around us were little jellyfish, floating out in a seemingly endless ether.

"This room is my favourite." Jasmine smiled and looked

up to the jellyfish above us. They didn't look real. They were ethereal. They looked two dimensional even.

"Why?" I asked.

"The colours are pretty," she replied. "And I mean, jellyfish are pretty cool to look at. Just floating there. It must be so peaceful."

"We should get home soon, shouldn't we?" I asked.

Jasmine nodded. "It's getting late. I know." She reached out for my hand and gave it a soft squeeze. "Let's just stay here a little longer. Neither of us are in a rush, right? Let's just… enjoy this."

Smiling, I squeezed her hand back and we stood there. Awash in the gradually changing light hues of the jellyfish tank, hand in hand. As I watched the jellyfish floating in their empty space, I felt a pair of eyes on me. Out of the corner of my eye, I could see Jasmine watching me. When I turned back to her, she didn't look away embarrassed or anything. She just kept looking at me. In her eyes, I could see the reflections of the jellyfish floating.

"I'm sorry about everything that happened two years ago." Her voice was barely audible. If it weren't for it being so quiet in this room, I might not have ever heard her.

"Jasmine, it wasn't all your fault. A lot of it was on me too."

"It was just all those stupid late-night talks. All the anxieties and all the worries."

"I know," I said. I rested a hand on her shoulder and gave her a soft rub. "Anxiety is the foundation of falling apart."

She smiled at me, washed in blue light. I smiled back, washed in red light. I remembered reading somewhere about inertia and light waves and the expansion of the universe. How red and blue are the differentiating colours between things moving toward and away from you. Like, things rushing to and from, they get shifted on the colour spectrum. The lights in the jellyfish room turn blue again, slowly. And Jas-

220

mine and I move closer. She met me halfway and pressed her lips to mine and the lights shifted slowly back red. And then blue. And then red. And it felt like it never ended. Like it never would. I would have been okay with that. I would have been okay being stuck in a constant push and pull with her.

"I'm sorry," Jasmine said, stepping back a few steps. "I— You just broke up with your girlfriend. That wasn't right of me." She looked away and then snapped back to me. "You didn't do it because of me, did you?"

"Jasmine, no. It's not like that."

"Are you sure?" she questioned. She stepped toward me. "Just seemed like really convenient timing... maybe?"

"Maybe it was just the right time to do it," I replied. "I was unhappy. I've been unhappy."

"I just don't want to be the reason you lost someone who could have been your future," she said. She hung her head down and sighed. "I'm sorry, Dee. I shouldn't have offered you on this adventure with me."

"The adventure still isn't over, Jasmine."

"Maybe it should be." She pulled on her hair a little bit and pushed it all back, freeing her face from stray hairs. "Aren't you even like a little upset about her?"

"It'll hit me tomorrow," I told her. "Please stop worrying about me. Let's just enjoy our adventure tonight and I'll deal with my emotions tomorrow. Okay?"

Jasmine sighed. "Fine."

"Okay." I smiled a little. I could still feel her warmth on my lips. Maybe she just feels guilty, like she stole me back or something. I guess that makes sense in this context. "Where to next?" I asked her.

She put her thumb to her lip and thought for a second. "I know what next."

Somehow we ended up in the market again in front of a produce stand. Why a produce stand was still open so late into the night, I'll never truly understand. But yet, there we stood.

Jasmine was gazing upon the selection of, you guessed it, cabbages. She needed a new Fred. So I happily obliged to help her find one.

Once we selected our new Fred, we made our way back to her apartment. It was quiet. I don't think anyone had come back at all in the few hours we had been gone, which meant the place was all Jasmine's for the night.

"We should have gotten more cheesecake balls," she said as she put the new Fred in the fridge.

I laughed. "Please, no more. Those cheesecake balls probably filled my daily calories for the next week."

"But where they or where they not worth it?"

I smiled and hung my head a bit. "Yeah. Yeah, they were worth it."

"Um, also… Are you staying the night?" Jasmine asked.

"Did you want me to?"

"Um." She looked around a little panicked for a second. "I guess it's up to you. Do you wanna stay here? I can get blankets and a pillow for you?"

"I can head home."

"But it's started to rain," she said, pointing to the window. Indeed, it had started to rain, but it was only supposed to be spitting until nine in the morning. I could stay, maybe.

"Should I stay though?"

Jasmine started pacing. "I don't know. I missed you so I want to spend more time with you, but I know you're thinking it's weird now with the whole you breaking up with your girlfriend five minutes before we kissed and stuff." She walked to the window and sighed. "Yeah. Maybe it's best for you to go home."

"I don't mind." I got up from the couch and walked to the front door. "You're welcome to text me whenever. Don't be a stranger."

"I won't," she said, turning back from the window and smiling at me. "Make sure you put on your coat." She pointed to a light coat I had been wearing earlier in the day. "Stay dry. Let me know when you make it home safe, okay?"

I nodded. "Of course. Go get some sleep." I gave her a soft smile and opened the front door.

"Dee."

I turned back to her, one foot in and one foot out of her apartment. "Yeah?"

She sniffled a bit. "I'm sorry. For everything. Disappearing for two years and all the other bullshit."

"Jasmine, it's okay."

"No, it's not." She sighed. "I'm an immature little girl still. I'm not ready for any of this. I still keep an imaginary friend."

"But it's Fred."

"He's a coping mechanism for loneliness, Dee."

I frowned a bit. "I guess if you cut it that way."

"No, that's what he is." Jasmine's eyes were sprouting small streams of tears down her face now. "I just don't know how to, like… *be* a person."

"Jasmine, you're figuring it out. You're okay."

"No, I'm not. I've been latching on to everyone that looks at me and it scares everybody away. You were the only person who I felt looked past my immaturities." She sniffled and took a long breath. "And then even you left me in the end."

I shut the door and stared at her. "It wasn't all you. I left because of my immaturities too. I didn't know how to deal with yours. I didn't know how to love from a distance. I always had nagging thoughts in my head that you were only pretending to want to still be with me, or that you were off talking to someone better. I had the same issues."

"But you handled them better," she stated.

"Obviously not. I broke up with you in just a few months."

"Maybe that was the right call to make."

"Why do you think that?"

She turned and shrugged. "I don't know!" Her voice got sharp. "Sometimes people just aren't made for each other.

223

Not every romance has a happy ending, maybe ours is one of those failures."

"If that were true, you wouldn't have kissed me tonight."

"Well, I—"

I raised my eyebrows and waited for a reply that never came. "Goodnight, Jasmine." I turned and walked out into the hallway, closing the door gently behind me.

The walk home was damp and cold and miserable. I kept thinking about the jellyfish room and the kiss and the red and the blue and the big fish tank and Fred and Jasmine and the summer camp and all of the everything in between the here and there.

I wished everything were simpler. But I think everybody wishes that. Life was never meant to be simple, and neither was love or friendship or working for a living. Life is hard. It's tough. Full of bullshit and confusing entanglements.

My apartment was empty when I got home. I'm very glad Samantha wasn't waiting here to entrap me and force me to rescind us breaking up. I didn't want to be with her anymore. I wasn't happy. I'd rather be alone and unhappy than let someone make me miserable.

Even in the next few days, I didn't really speak to anyone. I just went to and from work. I had only messaged Jasmine that night to tell her I got home and then we both went radio silent for a good few weeks. Like that night never happened. Maybe in her head it didn't. Maybe it shouldn't have.

THIRTY-FOUR

Sometimes, I think anyway, when we get closer and closer to a solution, the world seems to speed things up. Like tying the end of the knot to a story thread is like a whirlpool. At the start, it's very slow, but then once you're close to being done and submerged, you're spinning rapidly around and around.

It had been four weeks since that night with Jasmine. Now it's a Sunday. I invited Taron over since we didn't have class or work the next day and wanted to catch up. We don't ever seem to have matching time off anymore, which is sad.

"Seth's doing good," Taron replied. He was answering my question about our mutual friend Seth, you see, because Seth and I have been on conflicting schedules lately and never have time to talk anymore. It's pretty shitty.

"Is he writing or has he quit?"

"He still writes short stories from time to time," Taron replied. "Mostly, he writes scary stuff that he posts on some forum. But I'd rather that than the alternative."

"Which is?"

"Fanfiction?" Taron laughed softly. "Imagine him writing that shit." Taron's eyes lit up quickly. "Whoa! I bet we could convince him!"

"Wouldn't be too hard." We laughed about it. Seth was always down to write weird shit these days it seems.

"What about Jasmine?"

"What about her?" I asked, lolling my head around a bit and rolling my eyes at him.

"Well, have you seen her lately?"

"I actually did see her the other day."

"And what happened when you saw her?"

"She kissed me."

"Can you explain that to me again?" Taron asked. "You say she kissed you?"

"She did," I said. "I think. It's hard to tell. Maybe I kissed her."

"You know, I've heard kissing takes two, so maybe it was *both* of you who kissed each other at the same time. Kissing shouldn't be something that gets blamed on someone, you bozo."

"Ah, man, yeah, you're so smart actually." I laughed softly and tossed him another cola. "The whole point is that I'm still confused by it."

"She clearly still wants you." Taron looked at me and shot daggers. "And you clearly want to be with her too. So… what's the problem?"

"She's the problem." I sat down next to him on my couch. "And I guess I am too. We're both kinda messed up about each other. I think there's a lot of anxiety still there about how we don't really know how to *be* with each other."

"But you want to be?"

"Yes."

"And she wants to be?"

"Yes."

Taron clapped his hands together and looked at me, puzzled. "Then… what's the problem? Because you two want this to be easy? Relationships aren't easy. They're built on compromise and communication. They're hard work. But it's worth it for the right person. Do you think there's a chance you two are the right people for each other?"

I groaned. "I'm not sure, that's the problem. I don't wanna just try to pursue her and end up hurting us both more in the end."

"You were both pretty young and inexperienced before. Not to say you're any smarter now, I guess. But you have no reason not to try this again." Taron raised an eyebrow. "The universe has given you a second chance. Don't let it slip away. Most people never get a second chance."

"And what if turns out the same way?"

"Don't let it be for a lack of trying." He looked at the time on his watch. "Also, how long has the pizza been in the oven?"

"Oh, shit," I shouted, running to the oven. I pulled the pizza out and it was only mildly crispy. "I saved it."

Taron got up and walked over. "Just needs a fresh sprinkling of parmesan and it's good." He sliced the pizza up. "When was the last time you said you talked to Jasmine?"

I shrugged. "Three or four weeks by now." I take a slice of pizza off the pan and take a bite.

Taron rolls his eyes and lets out a deep sigh. He takes his slice and sits atop the counter. "You should text her."

"Right now?"

"I think she's still up. She's a writer, right? We're known to have terrible insomnia and drinking problems and all those other good things that keep us up at night."

I rolled my eyes a little and pulled up my phone. "Hey," I typed. "I know it's been a while, but you popped into my head so I wanted to say hi." Sent. Waited. Ate another slice of pizza. Taron and I chatted about the weather getting colder.

My phone dinged. "Hi." Another ding. "I've been thinking about you too, actually." Another ding. "I don't like how we left things and how we stopped talking... again."

"Me either," I wrote back, turning off my ringer sounds to save Taron from the annoyance.

"I've been thinking about some stuff we said to each other. About the anxieties and all that." Her message rang inside my head as I watched the typing notification bubbles jump up and down. "And, I guess, I dunno... I think we were brought back together for a reason. Maybe. Or not. Maybe that's dumb."

"It's not," I typed. "Taron said the same thing to me tonight, actually."

"I still feel guilty about you and your girlfriend."

"I promise it wasn't your fault. I haven't spoken to her in three weeks since she picked up her stuff from my place."

"Okay." There's a pause before she sent the next message. "I still think about that kiss too."

"Me too," I told her.

"I wish it had been longer."

"I wish that too."

She sent a sad emoji. "Maybe next time?"

I smiled softly. "Can we maybe see each other tonight?" I held my breath and watched the bubbles dancing on my screen waiting for her message back to me.

My phone vibrated in my hand. "You'll have to come find me."

THIRTY-FIVE

Taron was fine to stay at my apartment for the night by himself. He was tired anyway, so I let him stay and sleep while I set off into the night to find Jasmine. I had my idea of where she could have wound up. Either the cabbage kiosk at the market, the cheesecake ball kiosk, or the aquarium. All of those options are relatively close together, so it wouldn't be hard to find her.

Walking around the market by myself was a weird experience. I felt a thousand eyes on me, but yet nobody was staring or even paying me any mind at all. I stuck out like a sore thumb. I wondered how often Jasmine really came here. Did she actually spend a lot of time here? Or in the aquarium? Everybody has their own favourite places. I guess this, like certain sections of the writing camp, were among Jasmine's favourites.

I made my way to the cabbage kiosk and saw no Jasmine. Frowning slightly, I continued my walk across the market towards the cheesecake ball kiosk. When I got there, I order a bag of five and snacked on them while I walked to what realistically should have been my first stop on the search for Jasmine.

As I walked, I wondered about our journey together, Jasmine and I. At the camp, I at least felt pretty sure she would be the one for me. Something about her felt *right*. Like she was made for me. All that cliché romantic shit felt like the truth with her. And then as soon as there was an obstacle, it was a problem. Maybe it was our inexperience. The lack of foresight. The whatever. The this and the that. But maybe Taron was right after all: We had a second chance to do this right. To give each other an honest chance at being something real.

But looking back, we never even left the honeymoon stage of our relationship. A few months, a lot of good memories, and a summer filter on top of it all. Everything was *too* perfect. Everything felt *too* good for it to be the real thing. I've been told before in life that real love isn't easy. Great things take time; they have to flourish and mature and grow and be worked on. Day and night, you work together to keep sowing a garden of love and trust and compassion and a future together.

And then, Jasmine and I never got the chance to work on those things, to grow our gardens, to plant the seeds for our future. We quit on each other. We both lacked trying and it broke us mere weeks after we had the distance between us and when we were both more focused on school and enjoying our senior years and getting ready for the next step of life. Sometimes, to move forwards, we have to leave people behind. But I didn't want to leave her behind.

I approached the aquarium's back door with a thousand thoughts still in my head. Should I try again with Jasmine? Or would it be better to just let ourselves forget each other? Would it be more painful to break up in two years than to just let go now?

I wish I could just stop the story here and let it hang on the cliff forever.

But you made it this far. I might as well tell you how it ends.

The door creaked open and I made my way down the sketchy stairwell. Just as dimly lit as the other night, only this time the lobby was also dimly lit. No bright lights to guide me. I looked around and called out, but there was no one to answer me. The door into the aquarium, however, had been left open. I walked through it and followed the hallway into the room with the big tank of fish. I was expecting Jasmine to be there, ogling at the fish inside, but the room was empty.

But I figured, if Jasmine was here in the aquarium, she'd still be here. So I sat down and looked at the big tank of fish. I noticed a small notebook on the bench next to me. It would have to be Jasmine's. I opened it and saw a few familiar scribbles. It was the notebook we used at camp. My poems. Her poems. Some of Taron's drawings. Seth's musings. It was our story of that summer. She had even written stories of our adventures with Fred in the cabbage patch. The last page, however, was empty save for the title. *How does it end?*

"I don't know," I whispered, leafing through the notebook. "I wish I knew."

I set the notebook back down and looked back at the fish tank. I maybe sat there for too long. Maybe not long enough. There's not really a correct amount of time to sit and watch a fish tank though, is there?

After a little while, I got up from the bench and took the notebook. I walked further into the depths of the aquarium. Some of the tanks weren't fully lit up anymore. Not in the same way they should have been at least, just very soft lights. Maybe I wasn't meant to stop here. I made my way to the stingray tank and sat on another one of the benches to watch the "sea pancakes" fly around in the water.

On the bench next to me... was not another notebook. It

was nothing. I stopped here just to watch the stingrays float around for a while. Something about the careless way they glided around seemed so ethereal to me. I wish I could be a stingray. I wish I could float on forever.

Again, I spent more time than I should have sitting and watching a big tank of water and fish. I got up and continued on my way to the next room. The jellyfish tank. I could see the blue and red lights shifting slowly between each other as I walked up. And then her silhouette, perfectly outlined with the wall of glass and the endless watery gaze just on the other side.

"I've been waiting for you," her voice said softly as I approached her.

"I know," I said, stepping up beside her. "I've been looking for you."

"I know." She turned her head to me and smiled softly. "Took you longer than I thought it would have."

"I stopped for cheesecake balls."

She smiled wider and rolled her eyes a little, focusing back on the jellyfish tank. "I should have figured you would have. It's okay. I got some on my way here too."

"I figured you would have."

"So why'd you require my presence here?" I asked. "The jellyfish weren't making good conversation, huh?"

"Well." She let the air hang for a few seconds and then shrugged. "I've just been thinking about us a lot. Like, the kiss. And the years apart. And how within a day of talking, we had a kiss. I dunno."

"I know. I get it. I've been thinking a lot too."

"And it's just weird, you know?"

I nodded. "I do."

The room fell silent again and neither of us knew what to say next. We both were thinking the same things at a mile a minute. The anxieties of two years ago, the rushed feeling of three weeks ago, the kiss that didn't last nearly long enough, and so much more. Like she had said, maybe we were brought back together for a reason. Maybe the universe was giving us the second chance we needed to make this something real and concrete.

"Dee."

"Jasmine."

"Would you be opposed to trying again?"

I smiled softly and gave her a quick look out of the corner of my eye. Neither of us had made eye contact with each other yet tonight. "I wouldn't be opposed, no."

"Do you think we were meant to be here? In this spot? On this night?"

"Like, destiny?"

"Yeah."

I exhaled sharply. "Maybe." I turned back to the jellyfish. "But maybe not. Maybe destiny is our own doing. We're only here because we both made plans to come to the same school in the first place."

"We manifest our own destiny now." She laughed softly. "You knew I was avoiding you completely all last year, right?"

"I had my suspicions."

She sighed. "I just couldn't bear to see you. I was still hurt about our situation and then I saw you with your girlfriend occasionally around campus and then I knew it was useless to try to talk to you then."

"So what changed?" I asked.

"You finally saw me first."

"I guess."

"The last two years have been weird," she stated. "This was probably around the same time we broke up, I think. Two years ago."

I chewed at my lip. "Yep. My biggest mistake."

"Well, I know I'm two years late on this, but I wish you'd take me back." She finally turned and caught my eyes. Reflecting the colours of the room, red and blue. She smiled softly. "If you would like to have me back, that is?"

"I would love that."

"I would too." She smiled wide and got a little teary-eyed. "I've missed you, Dee. I really have."

"There wasn't a day I didn't wonder about you," I told her. "I've missed you just as much. I want to give us a real shot at this. Me, you, and Fred."

Jasmine lunged forward and wrapped her arms tightly around me. "Me, you, and Fred." She squeezed as tight as she could. All I could smell was her perfume. (Some kind of flower mixed with a soft vanilla.)

"We should probably go see him. We didn't hire a babysitter," I told her.

She laughed. "What a cheesy way to get into my apartment."

"Well, it's better to hide the intention, no?"

"No!" She pushed away from me with a big smile on her face. "I want you to want me."

"Oh, I do."

She smirked at me and nodded her head towards the exit. "So then let's go."

The blue lights washed over us one last time as we started moving and I felt as though the universe was indeed rushing towards me all at once. Jasmine and I, rushing towards each other for the past two years, slowly, but from a distance. Did it make sense in some faux cliché "I was feeling blue" kind of way? Is that the blue shift metaphor I'm going with? Yes. Yes, it is.

But that's it. That's the end of the story. Me, Jasmine, and Fred. I can't help but wonder if maybe the universe did bring us together. Or maybe it was Fred. After all, we were kind of like his adoptive parents, right? Maybe he did his best to bring us back together in the end. Maybe it was Taron. Maybe it was nothing. I guess it doesn't really matter now.

Happy ever after.

About the Author

Darren Richardson is, of the time of writing this, a young adult. A young adult that enjoys writing, napping, gaming, drinking coffee, staying up late, and learning things.

When it comes to writing Darren likes to write about teen fiction, teen romance, young adult fiction, general fiction, fantasy, crime, and really anything else he feels up for. He finds the most challenging part of writing to be getting the motivation to keep going when you're already halfway through a novel.

As Darren gets older, he hopes to still be writing and creating things in every facet of media and art that he can. His advice for writers, young and old, is to just keep writing. Even when it feels like you're completely tapped out of words, keep trying to get something written. Every word is one step closer to a finished product.

Made in the USA
Middletown, DE
08 December 2020